Mail Order Motherhood

Book eight in the Brides of Beckham
Kirsten Osbourne

Prologue

ELIZABETH MILLER TOOK a deep sniff of the beautiful summer air. It was hot, but she didn't mind. She was off work for a change and she'd sneaked away from her family. She sighed. She'd never really understood why their younger brothers and sisters had made Susan so crazy. Yes, they had always annoyed her, but they hadn't made her want to hurt them. Now that she was the oldest at home? She wanted to hurt each and every one of them on a daily basis. Why couldn't they act human?

She was on her way to town to mail a letter to Susan, her older sister. Susan had moved away a year before to be a mail order bride, and now lived happily with her husband and four sons in Fort Worth, Texas of all places. She wondered how Susan would react if she just showed up on her doorstep and said she couldn't handle the "demon horde" any longer. She chuckled as she imagined how her sister would respond.

The good people of their church had nicknamed their younger brothers and sister the demon horde years ago, and she fully understood why. They were hellions, each and every one of them.

Elizabeth didn't walk fast, because she was in no hurry to go back home. She would go to the post office and mail her letter, and then maybe she'd go to the mercantile and look around. She hadn't been there in a while. She had days off so rarely that it was time she took full advantage. She felt a touch of guilt that she hadn't told her mother she wasn't working that day, but she was so happy to finally be able to get away, she tried to ignore the guilt.

When she got to the post office, she heard a familiar voice from the front of the line. When the woman turned around, limping toward her, she knew she was right. "Mrs. Long!"

The older woman stopped in front of Elizabeth and smiled. "Susan Miller's sister. Elizabeth? Is that right?"

Elizabeth smiled and nodded. "You're good with names."

"Sometimes I am. I try to be." Harriett Long was flipping two letters in her hands over and over.

"I'm mailing a letter to my sister now. She's so happy. Thank you for what you did for her. I'm so happy there's a mail order bride service in our town to help people who need it." Elizabeth stepped to the front of the line and gave the post mistress her letter. "Anything for my family?"

The post mistress smiled and handed her a letter. "You got another letter from Susan."

Elizabeth clutched the letter to her chest and saw Harriett was still standing there waiting for her. She held up her letter. "I got one from Susan!" She got weekly letters from her sister, but she was thrilled for each one.

Harriett smiled. "I'm glad. She seems really happy when I hear from her."

"Oh, she is. You really changed her life." Elizabeth stepped out of the post office and breathed deeply, smiling happily. "I love days off." She looked around the town and wondered what she wanted to do with her time.

"Would you like to have a piece of pie next door?" Harriett asked. There was a small café beside the post office where she had stopped to eat with several of her brides over the time she'd been running her business.

Elizabeth nodded. "That sounds fine. I have all day to do whatever I want, but my parents don't know I'm off, so I need to be gone all day."

Harriett laughed, linking her arm through Elizabeth's. "Let's have lunch then."

She led Elizabeth to the small café, and they sat down at a table in the corner. "How's business going?" Elizabeth asked once they'd ordered their food. She'd been fascinated by the mail order bride business Harriett ran since she'd met the other woman.

"It's going really well, but I'm about to have to close it. I'm going to be a mail order bride myself."

Elizabeth gawked at Harriett for a moment before shaking her head. "You can't close the business! What about the women who need a way out? They need to be able to do something." She bit her lip. "I'm thrilled for you, though."

"Thank you." Harriett shrugged. "I agree about the business, but I'm moving to Seattle."

Elizabeth sighed, looking down at the table. "I'm really happy for you. I'm just sad for the women of Beckham." She'd heard stories about other women in the area being able to leave and be happy thanks to Harriett's services. She really felt like the town was better off for having a mail order bride service there. "Do you have any friends who could take it over?"

Harriett shook her head. "I don't. I don't know who I would even ask." She sighed and suddenly her face lit up as she looked at Elizabeth. "What about you? Have you ever wanted to run a business?"

Elizabeth slowly shook her head. "I love the idea of being independent, but I live with my family. You know, the 'demon horde?' There's no way I could run a business with that kind of chaos going on around me."

Harriett seemed to think about the problem. "I was worried I was going to have to let all the servants in my house go. I'm taking my butler, Higgins, with me, but I need someone who will be willing to stay in the house. I can set up a fund that the money for household upkeep will come from. That way no one will have to find a new job, and you'll have a place to work."

Elizabeth stared at Harriett in shock. "Are you saying I can live in your beautiful house with no cost?"

Harriett laughed. "The cost will be learning to run my business and helping the women of Beckham."

"I'll have to speak to my parents, of course, but I love the idea. I won't be eighteen until October. Would you have a problem with me running it before I turn eighteen?"

"I won't. But I'll want to pick out a new butler for you. Someone who will be able to run any errands you need and take care of problems. Higgins can show him how to do the job before he goes."

Elizabeth smiled, her eyes bright. "I'd love to do it then. I can't think of anything that would make me happier than helping others."

Harriett squeezed Elizabeth's hand. "It's a deal then. Talk to your parents and come to me tomorrow. I leave in a month, and I want every minute of that time to talk to you about how I do things."

Chapter 1

ALBERT STARED DOWN at the burnt roast and wanted to scream. How many meals would he burn before he figured out how to make a simple dinner for his family? It was a good thing the local bakery kept stocked with bread, or his children would never have anything to eat. "Looks like we're having bread and jam again, kids." He walked to the door and tossed out the black meat.

"We like bread and jam, Papa," Gertrude insisted. Gertie was six, and she did her best around the house, but her mother had barely had a chance to teach her any homemaking skills before her death six months prior.

Robert, the youngest at four, nodded. "Bread and jam is good."

Albert sighed as he turned back to them. "I'm glad you think so. It's not exactly healthy for you, though."

He quickly cut several pieces of bread off the loaf from the work table and put them on a plate in the middle of the table along with butter and a jar of jam he'd picked up from the mercantile. They sat down, and he bowed his head praying over the meal. He watched as the children devoured the bread. Their manners had deteriorated a great deal since his wife had died as well. Why hadn't she lived long enough to see her children grown up? Why hadn't it been someone with no small children to raise?

As he ate his own meal, he thought again about the advertisement he'd seen in the paper. "Are you lonely? Not enough women to choose from? For a small fee, we'll send a mail order bride to you. Your expenses include her travel and spending money. Send a letter with your requirements to Harriett Long, General Delivery, Beckham, Massachusetts to inquire."

He looked at the little faces, now both covered in jam, and decided it was time. He couldn't keep trying to raise them on his own while running his ranch. It was just too hard. Gertrude watched over Robert all day, but he constantly worried about them, and rode back to the house several times a day, costing him valuable hours he could be working and mending fences before it got too cold. Montana wasn't known for staying warm year round after all.

After the dishes were done and the children tucked into bed, he sat down at the table and wrote a letter. He didn't know how long it would take, but two months was too long at this point. He needed a wife yesterday.

CLARA WALKED INTO BECKHAM, trying not to drag her feet. She needed to talk to the banker, and she knew his response wouldn't be favorable. When her husband had died two years before, she'd been sure that she could keep farming and make enough to support her and their two children. Now, she wasn't sure she could even face the banker. She had to ask for an extension, but she feared she already knew what his answer would be. He wasn't the kindest man in the world, and she knew she'd already tried his patience.

Clara had long dark hair and pretty brown eyes. She had full lips and her nose was uptilted slightly at the end, which had caused many girls in school to say she thought she was better than the rest of them. She never had felt that way, of course. She had lost a lot of weight since her husband had died and she'd taken over his farm responsibilities. There never seemed to be enough food anymore, and she was more worried about her children eating than she was about herself.

She'd put on her prettiest dress for this meeting, but that wasn't saying much. She'd had pretty clothes before Nathan had died, but she hadn't been able to afford new clothes since. She just couldn't consistently work as much of the land as he'd been able to. She didn't have the strength, and she still had her children to take care of.

She walked into the bank and smiled at the teller at the front. "He's waiting for you, Mrs. Baldwin," the young man said.

Clara walked to the back of the bank to the small office where she knew the bank manager would be waiting for her. She knocked once on the open door and took the chair he indicated. She waited for him to start the conversation, because he'd been the one to call her there.

"I'm sure you know why I've asked you here," Mr. Baxter said.

Clara sighed. "I'm not going to be able to pay the full amount this harvest. Can you give me an extension until this time next year?" She knew the answer. He'd told her last year that if she didn't pay it in full this October, she and her children would be out on their ears. She closed her eyes while she waited for his response, half expecting the man to start yelling at her.

He sighed and leaned back in his chair, shaking his head. "You know I can't do that. What kind of a businessman would I be if I kept extending loans to people who will obviously never be able to pay them back?"

Clara didn't say anything. She just played with the front of her dress, forming pleats and then laying them flat. What could she say?

"You'll need to have the full amount by the end of October, or I will be foreclosing on your land."

Clara stood and left his office. She knew no amount of tears would change his mind. Mr. Baxter was known for removing widows and orphans from land when money was owed. He had quite a reputation. She had a bit of money, and since she was going to be evicted, she decided to spend it to make a new dress for her daughter. The girl's dresses showed an indecent amount of calf, and now that she was ten, people were starting to look at her with disgust.

She walked into the mercantile and immediately went to the wanted ads on the back wall. She had to find a job she could do before she lost the farm. A job that would pay enough to support her and both children.

Most of the notices were for farm workers, and she knew she'd never make enough that way, even if someone would hire a woman. She quickly read over the different notices tacked there and stopped when she saw one that might work. "Mail Order Bride agency needs women who are looking for the adventure of their lives. Men out West need women to marry. Reply in person at 300 Rock Creek Road. See Miss Elizabeth Miller." The Millers went to her church, and she knew that the older daughter had been a mail order bride, but she'd had no idea Elizabeth had taken over the running of the agency.

She studied the address for a moment and set out before she lost her nerve. Surely somewhere in the west was a man who wanted to marry a thirty year old widow with a ten year old daughter and an eight year old son. Right?

Clara was surprised by the house she found when she reached the address. How was Elizabeth Miller able to afford to live here? She knocked on the door and held her breath while she waited. A young man in his mid-twenties came to the door. He had blond hair and blue eyes, but a formal manner. "May I help you?"

"Yes, I'm here to see Miss Miller. Tell her that Clara Baldwin is calling." She tried to act as if she visited houses like that one every day.

"Come inside." He led her down the hall to a door on the left. "Is Miss Miller expecting you?"

Clara shook her head. "No, she isn't." She hoped she was in and would see her.

He opened the door and said, "There's a Clara Baldwin here to see you, Miss Miller."

Elizabeth hurried to the door. "Mrs. Baldwin. It's good to see you." She indicated the couch behind her. "Come in and have a seat." Elizabeth's eyes were kind

Clara was astonished by the lack of surprise in Elizabeth's eyes. She'd known the girl since she was small. "I'm sure you're wondering why I've come to see you," Clara began.

Elizabeth shook her head. "Of course, I'm not. You need to find a way to support your family, or you need to marry a man who can do it for you. I'm very impressed you were able to support them for as long as you have without help."

Clara sighed, pleased that Elizabeth understood, and there was no censure in her eyes. "Is there someone you can send me to?" Clara hated the idea of leaving everyone she knew behind, but her children needed to be provided for.

Elizabeth turned to the desk she was sitting in front of and quickly flipped through the letters there. "I think this one would work well for you. He's in a similar situation."

Clara took the letter Elizabeth offered and quickly read through it. "Dear potential bride, I'm needing a woman who is willing and capable of managing a ranch house. I have two children, Gertrude and Robert, aged six and four respectively. My wife died and left me alone with them six months ago, and I must admit that I have no idea how to run a household or raise children. Sally did all of that for me. I would like a woman who is over twenty-five. I do not mind if she has been married before or if she has children. No more than four children please, because I already have my two. If you're willing to work hard and raise two children that are not your own, please send me a letter. I would like someone who is willing to move quickly as my children are not eating well, because I'm incapable of cooking a meal without burning it. I live in rural Montana and work a ranch. I'm not a rich man, but I can certainly afford a few more mouths to feed. Thank you. Albert Hanson."

Clara read over the letter again before looking up at Elizabeth. "Yes, he sounds like what I need." She thought wistfully of Nathan his smile on their wedding day. How would she be able to look at another man as her husband?

Elizabeth smiled. "I thought of you when I first read the letter."

"Really? You should have brought it to me!" Clara was shocked the younger woman had even thought about her but pleased as well.

"I just got it yesterday. I was planning on talking to you about it at church Sunday."

Clara sighed. "What's next? I've never been a mail order bride before."

"Well, first thing is writing him back. Are you in a hurry to get this done?"

"Yes, I have to be off the farm in sixty days or less." Clara was embarrassed to admit it, but it didn't seem to bother Elizabeth at all.

"That's a good amount of time to accomplish this in." Elizabeth handed Clara a pen and paper. "You write. I'm going to run and have tea and cookies sent in here." She left the room in a hurry, and Clara noticed the bell for summoning servants with a smile. Elizabeth was obviously not used to living in wealth. Clara felt a great deal more comfortable when she realized the other woman probably felt as out of place as she did.

She hurriedly wrote the letter and finished it after Elizabeth came back. Handing it to the younger woman, she sighed. "I have no idea how my children are going to feel about this."

Elizabeth shrugged. "I hope they'll be happy to have food to eat and decent clothes to wear."

Clara sighed. "I went to the mercantile to get fabric to make a new dress for Natalie, and forgot all about it when I saw your advertisement. I'll have to go back on my way home."

They ate the cookies and tea while Elizabeth talked about the whole mail order bride process. "Susan couldn't be happier. I thought it was strange that she ended up married to her groom's brother, but she seems content there. She's expecting."

Clara smiled. She'd always liked Susan. "How does she feel about that? I remember how she always felt about the 'demon horde.'" Clara had always hated the nickname given to the Miller children, but she certainly understood it.

"I think she's happy about it. She seems to be anyway. Her husband had four boys when they married, so it will be nice if they can have one of their own. She's hoping for a girl."

"Of course she is! With four boys a girl would be very welcome." Clara stood. "I need to go buy some fabric and head back to the farm. Thanks for the tea and cookies."

Elizabeth stood, smiling at the older woman. "I'm glad you came by. I'll run the return letter over to you as soon as I receive it."

"Thank you. I'd appreciate that. I'm going to keep working the farm and get as much as I can from the crop this year. Maybe I can go to my new husband with some clothes that haven't been patched twenty times."

"He'll send train tickets and a small amount of money for the trip. Don't worry too much about having your own."

Elizabeth walked Clara to the door and watched her walk away, hoping the older woman would be able to settle in well in her new home.

ALBERT LEFT THE CHILDREN in the wagon and hurried into the mercantile to check the mail. Billings was the biggest town around, but it was still small enough that there was no need for a post office. "Any mail for me?" He'd started checking last week. He could only spare one day a week to drive into town, so he checked while he was there buying bread and jam.

Samuel handed him a letter. "Got this one."

Albert looked at the return address and opened the letter. Two letters fell out for him. One from the owner of the agency, but the other was the one he focused on as he walked back to the wagon. "Dear Albert, My name is Clara Baldwin, and I'm a twenty-eight year old widow. I have a daughter who is ten and a son who is eight. I've been widowed for two years and trying to keep up the farm that my husband worked until his death. The three of us need a fresh start. I enjoy cooking, and would love to be just a housewife again, instead of a housewife and a farmer. My children are hard workers as well, and we would work hard for you. I'm not beautiful, but so far no small children have run away screaming upon seeing my face. I await your reply. Yours, Clara."

Albert smiled at the words and carefully thumped the letter against his thigh. She'd do. He walked back to the front of the mercantile and quickly wrote a letter back before going to the train station. He bought three tickets for three weeks later leaving from Beckham, Massachusetts and arriving in Billings, Montana. He wasn't looking forward to having a wife and two new children, but he was looking forward to having a clean house and good meals again.

He mailed his letter, payment for the service, train tickets, and a small amount of money to help his future wife with her food during the trip before leaving Billings. On the way home, he carefully explained what he'd done to his children. "When your mama died, she left us with no one to cook or clean for us. I keep trying, but I'm just not good at it." He sighed. "I'm sending back East for a wife to come and take care of us. The one I found has two children."

Gertie looked up at him. "So we won't have bread and jam for every meal anymore?"

He shook his head. "No, your new mama will cook and clean and teach you to do both of those things as well. She'll be here in a little over a month." He hoped the children would understand that he wasn't replacing their mother, but just having someone come to take care of them.

Gertie nodded, putting her arm around Robert. "That sounds good, Papa. We'll keep taking care of each other until then."

Nothing else was said as they made the hour drive to their home north of Billings. As they pulled into the yard, Albert looked around thinking about how little he'd done to keep up the house that summer. The vegetable plot lay fallow, and the house needed a fresh coat of paint. He just didn't have time to worry about it, though. He had to get the rest of the fences mended before the bad weather came on them. The snows could start in November or they could start in September. He hoped that November would be the answer, but you just never knew in Montana.

She sounded like she was a strong woman, to be able to keep her children on her own for two years after her husband's death, but she'd have to be very strong to survive through the winters here. He said a quick prayer, asking that God make her stronger than she already was so she could make it through.

He took the children into the house and gave Gertie orders to watch her brother. "I'm going to unhitch the team and get to work. You take care of your brother now."

"Yes, Papa." Gertie stood beside her brother holding his hand. She made it clear that she knew her job was to take care of him.

He gave her a nod of encouragement before leaving to go out and mend fences close to the house. There just weren't any neighbors close enough that he could take the time to leave them with others. He hoped his wife knew how to read and write well, because the children would need to be taught at home as well. There were no schools close enough to learn in.

He put the team into the stable and saddled his favorite riding horse. Swinging up onto her back, he rode out onto the range toward the border that was closest to the house. He'd mend this fence today.

His new wife would be there soon. He hoped she understood when he put her in the same bedroom as her daughter. He couldn't have a new love in his life, not even with how much he needed a wife and mother for his children. He would feel like he was cheating on his wife.

Sally had contracted a wasting disease. She'd gotten weaker and weaker. He took her into town to see the doctor, but he'd said there was nothing he could do. She was dying. She'd been gone four months later. His Sally had been a beautiful woman, and he missed her every day. They'd grown up in Texas, but she hadn't liked the heat. So they'd made the move from Texas to become Montana ranchers as soon as they'd married. He wondered if they'd been stupid to make the trip. He berated himself every day, thinking she'd have lived if they'd just stayed in Texas.

He shook his head, and jumped down from his horse once he realized where he was. It was time to work. He couldn't risk losing his cattle this winter. He'd have three extra mouths to feed.

Chapter 2

CLARA CAREFULLY PACKED her dishes into the barrel she'd purchased for them. She didn't have much more time to leave, and she'd stay with her parents as soon as she'd sold everything off. Just for a little while, though. They'd made it clear they couldn't afford to feed three extra mouths on an ongoing basis. The buyers for the dishes would be there soon.

She looked around her small kitchen. The oven and work tables had already been sold. The kitchen table was gone. The room was almost empty. Just the dishes and the pots and pans were left. The pots and pans would be sold the following day, and she'd be required to move at that point. She sighed. She hated the idea of giving up her independence and moving in with her parents. She'd been on her own for far too long.

She was startled by a knock on the door, and checked the clock still hanging on the wall. The buyer for the dishes was already there? They were two hours early!

She opened the door wide. "Oh, Elizabeth. Come in." She hadn't been expecting the other woman to come with a response so quickly. She guessed it was just a social call.

Elizabeth stepped into the kitchen and looked around. "You've got almost everything packed up."

Clara nodded. "We're all moving in with my parents tonight." She sighed. "They're complaining about how much we'll cost them, but I'll have a little bit of money to help out with bills in case Albert doesn't want me."

Elizabeth held out a letter. "That's why I'm here. I have a letter for you." Her eyes were bright with excitement.

Clara wiped her hands on her apron and took the letter. She opened it, obviously nervous about what was inside. "Dear Clara, You sound like you're just what we're looking for. I've enclosed train tickets for you and your children. I will meet you at the station in Billings, and we'll have an hour drive from there. I'll have both my children with me. I'm tall and have dark hair. We'll marry before we leave town. I look forward to meeting you and your children. Yours, Albert."

She looked at the train tickets included and saw they left in three days. She breathed a sigh of relief when she saw the money he'd included as well. She could give the money she'd made selling everything to her parents for the inconvenience of having her and the children for three nights, and then she could use the money he'd sent for the things she'd need. She mentally calculated. There would be enough to give her parents something even if she used a bit of the money for fabric for new clothes. She and Natalie both needed a lot of new things, and so did Clarence. She sighed. She'd give her parents as much as she could.

"Thank you, Elizabeth. Our train leaves in three days." Clara smiled at the younger woman as best she could. She didn't want her to think she wasn't grateful for the help, but honestly? She had no desire to go to Montana of all places.

Elizabeth squeezed Clara's hand as if she understood the words that weren't spoken. "I'll see you off at the train station. What time does your train leave?"

Clara glanced at the tickets again. "Nine in the morning."

"I'll meet you there at half past eight."

"You don't need to see me off. I'll be there with the children." Clara couldn't imagine why the younger woman would want to be there.

Elizabeth shook her head. "I'll be there. Do you need anything before I go?"

"No. I'll see you before we leave." Clara went back to packing, hoping that the people purchasing her dishes would hurry. She had to shop for some fabric for new clothes for her children now.

When the children came in from school, Clara told them the next day would be their last. "We're leaving first thing Monday morning to go to Montana. There's a man there that I'll marry. He has two children." She watched her children's faces as she told them her big news. She didn't expect them to be pleased, but she hoped they wouldn't be terribly upset.

Natalie gaped at her. "You're marrying a stranger?"

Clara straightened her spine. "Yes, I'm marrying a stranger. I don't really have a choice in the matter. We're losing the farm and have nowhere to go."

Natalie's eyes filled with tears. "But all my friends are here."

"You'll make new friends." Clara looked down at her hands, feeling like she was doing something horrible for her daughter, but knowing there was no real choice. "I'm sorry, Natalie. I really don't have a choice." She hugged her daughter, noticing the stiff way the girl held herself against her.

"I want to stay with Grandma and Grandpa!" Natalie insisted.

"You can't. You have to come with me." Clara had no doubt her parents wouldn't let their granddaughter stay anyway.

Clarence poked Natalie. "You need to listen to Mama. We have to go to Montana." Clarence had always dreamed of going west and being a cowboy. This was something he wanted to do.

Listening to Natalie whine and complain about having to move grated on Clara's nerves until she finally told the girl she didn't want to hear another word. She was ten years old and too old to be complaining about things she should be able to understand.

They walked to her parents' house that night, and when they arrived, Clara carefully explained they would only be there for three days. She gave her mother fifteen dollars to pay for any food they'd eat while they were there and make up for the inconvenience of having them.

Alice Johnson shook her head. "It's not the money, dear. It's that you didn't plan well." She shoved the money back at Clara. "You should be able to support yourself and your children without our help."

Clara refused to meet her mother's eyes. "I'll be going to the mercantile tomorrow, and I'll need to sew up until we leave. I'd rather you kept the money." She couldn't believe how unsupportive her mother was being. She hadn't expected her husband to die young. How could she have?

She helped with the dishes that night, while the children made themselves scarce. Clara knew that Natalie was going to try to get her mother alone while they were there, and she decided to cut her off at the pass. "I think Natalie is going to ask you if she can live here with you while Clarence and I go on to Montana. I want you to tell her 'no.'"

Alice sighed. "I'll tell her you said to tell her no."

Clara took a deep breath, determined to hold her temper. "I want the 'no' to come from you, Mother. She needs to understand that she's not going to be allowed to come back here to live with you if she doesn't like Montana."

"Why are you taking her to Montana if you know she won't like it?"

Clara turned on her mother. "Why do you think I'm taking her there? I've been working night and day for two years trying to make the farm work for me. I have nowhere to live and nowhere to go. I'm marrying a total stranger so my children will have food to eat and a roof over their heads. I'm doing the best I can for them!"

Alice shook her head. "You shouldn't have married beneath you the way you did."

"Beneath me?" Clara put the last dish away and slowly put the towel she'd used to dry the dishes on the counter. "Good night, Mother.

Please remember what I said. Tell Natalie she's not welcome to stay here with you."

Clara climbed the stairs to her childhood bedroom she'd be sharing with Natalie for the next two days. Clarence was across the hall from them. She sat down on the edge of the bed. "Do you want to go to school tomorrow or do you want to go to the mercantile with me to choose fabric for your new dresses?"

Natalie's eyes lit up. "New dresses?" She hadn't had new dresses in years, not since her father had died. "May I help you pick out fabric?"

Clara smiled and put her arm around her daughter's shoulders. "I'd like that a lot. We can make them together this weekend as well."

THE DAYS PASSED WITH a flurry of activity. Every minute she wasn't helping her mother, Clara was in the tiny bedroom she was sharing with Natalie working on dresses. She made Natalie's first and decided to hold off on her own. Hers were at least decent if not a little worn. Natalie's were much too short and tight, and desperately needed to be thrown into the rag bag.

When Monday morning dawned, she said goodbye to her parents at breakfast. "I'll write when I arrive so you'll know how to reach me, and you'll know we're okay," she promised.

Her father nodded slowly. "I hope this man isn't a farmer like Nathan."

Clara bit her lip. Nathan had been a good husband and father, and she'd loved him, despite how her parents felt about him. "He's a rancher."

"A rancher? That's not much better than a farmer." William frowned at her.

Clara shrugged. "I didn't have a lot of choices. Men don't beat down the doors of widows begging them for their hands so they can shower them with gifts and affection." She stood. "Thank you for allowing us to stay these past few days." She wished she didn't have to be so formal, but she didn't feel like she could be anything else with them.

Her father drove her into town to help her with the trunk she was taking. She had finished two dresses for Natalie, and she planned on making at least one dress for herself on the trip. Clarence had more clothes, because her brother had a son who was just older than Clarence, and he got his old clothes. They weren't in perfect shape, and she'd have to make some more soon, but she wouldn't be embarrassed if they weren't done when she got to Montana.

At the train station, Elizabeth sat beside Clara while the children sat across from them. Natalie looked pretty in her new dress, but she looked angry with the world. Clarence looked excited. None of them had ever been on a train before, and he was the only one excited about it.

"I wanted to have a quick talk with you before you go," Elizabeth told her. She'd given her a canvas bag full of sandwiches for the trip, which Clara was thrilled with. She didn't want to spend all of Albert's money before she arrived in Montana.

Clara turned her attention from her pouting daughter to Elizabeth. "Of course."

"I want you to know if Albert isn't who he seems you don't have to marry him. You'll have a place here. If he...hurts you in anyway, you need to just come home." Elizabeth stumbled over the words as if she'd been told she needed to say them, but felt uncomfortable doing so.

Clara shook her head. "I have no home any longer. I'll stay no matter what."

Elizabeth shook her head. "If anything happens, if he hits you, I want you to come back here. I will find you a job, and you'll have a place to live with me until you're settled." She kept her voice in a whisper so the children wouldn't hear her, but her voice was adamant.

Clara stared at her for a moment, before slowly nodding. "I'll come back if he hits me."

Elizabeth looked relieved and gave Clara a one-armed hug. "Write to me when you get there to let me know you're okay."

Clara nodded. "I'll do that." She couldn't help but wonder why the younger woman cared, but she wouldn't turn down a place to stay if her marriage was bad.

The conductor called out their train, and Clara got to her feet. She'd seen trains before but had never really thought about what it would be like to ride on one. She stared up at the huge machine and tried not to show her fear in front of her children. "Thank you for all your help," she told Elizabeth before motioning the children to go before her to get to the train.

They found seats together, with Clarence sitting across from Clara and Natalie. Clara immediately leaned down to take out the pieces of the dress she was making for herself. She'd carefully cut it out before leaving her mothers, but she needed to do all the sewing on the train. She offered two pieces to Natalie to work on to give the girl something to do during the long hours they'd have until the first stop, but Natalie shook her head, refusing to even look at her.

Clara sighed. It was going to be a long trip.

IT TOOK A FULL WEEK to reach Montana with a long stop in Chicago to switch trains. Clara had been convinced she'd lose one or both of her children in the big city, but they'd all managed to wash a bit and find their way to the other train. Clara kept up her sewing. She was able to make two dresses and an apron before they pulled into the station in Billings.

"I don't know why you're bothering with a new apron, Mama. You're just going to get it dirty again." Natalie's voice had been a constant whine in her ear through the trip, and Clara was ready to scream.

"I'm not starting a new marriage with an old dirty apron."

Natalie had rolled her eyes at her mother, but not another word had been said on the subject of aprons.

They got off the train together, Clara's eyes looking out over the faces wondering which face was the one that was waiting for her. Finally, she spotted a tall man with dark hair and eyes off to the side of the platform who was holding the hands of a young girl and boy. She lifted her hand in a slight wave, trying to verify that he was the one they were looking for.

The man nodded at her and walked in her direction, indicating he must be the one who was waiting for her and her children. She walked toward him, finding his face hard. There didn't seem to be any welcome on his face at all. Was he not Albert?

When they reached one another, she smiled and said, "Albert?" He gave a quick nod, saying nothing, just taking her bags from her. "We have to collect our trunk as well," she told him.

He nodded, walking toward the area where trunks and large items were being distributed to their rightful owners. His children stayed with her, and she smiled down at them. The girl was staring up at her with wide gray eyes, and she seemed almost frightened. "Are you Gertrude?" Clara asked.

The girl nodded. She pointed to her brother. "This is Robert."

"It's nice to meet you both. This is my daughter, Natalie, and my son, Clarence. I'm Clara."

Gertrude nodded. "Papa said you were here to be our new mama."

"That's right. I am. Natalie and Clarence will be your new sister and brother."

"Okay." Clara started them all walking in the direction Albert had taken. She nodded at Clarence. "Go see if you can help with our trunks."

Clarence hurried ahead, going to catch up with Robert and offer to help. She watched as Albert and Clarence carefully lifted the trunk down together and carried it to an old farm wagon. It was just like the one she'd used back home, so it was a welcome sight. It was late September, and the weather was already nippy. She hoped they wouldn't be out too late that evening.

When she reached the wagon, Albert helped her up, before climbing in beside her while the four children climbed in the back, Clarence sitting atop the trunk to better see the town. Natalie still had her look of defiance on her face, but Clara was grateful that she was saying nothing as she sat with the other children.

Clara looked down at her old dress, wishing she'd had time to change into one of the new ones she'd just made. This one was gray and had seen better days. "We're going straight to the preacher's house," Albert said. They were the first words he'd said to her, and she was almost startled to hear his deep voice.

"Will there be time before the ceremony for me to change into a new dress? I'd rather not get married in this one," she said. She wished she dared ask for a hot bath first, but she wouldn't cause another woman that much work.

"Then why'd you wear it?" he asked, obviously exasperated by her question.

She looked down, staring at the tips of her shoes. "I've been wearing the same dress for a week since we left Massachusetts. I haven't really had an opportunity to change."

He nodded curtly. "We'll ask the pastor's wife." He said nothing else about how hard her journey must have been. When they arrived, he helped her down from the wagon, and she picked up the carpet bag at her feet with her new dress in it.

The new dress was lavender with tiny flowers on it. She'd thought it looked so pretty when she'd finished it the previous evening, and now she didn't even feel like putting it on for the first time. She was marrying an angry, unhappy man. What had she gotten herself into?

The children followed behind them, and she was whisked away to the pastor's bedroom by the pastor's wife so she could quickly change her dress. "Thank you so much for letting me change in here."

Mrs. Simpson smiled at her. "It's no problem. I wouldn't want to have to marry in that dirty old dress either."

Clara blushed, knowing the woman couldn't have meant the words the way they sounded. She rushed to change her clothes and straightened her hair. She'd have given everything she owned for a bath just then, but there was no doubt in her mind that was too much to ask.

She hurried back into the parlor where the pastor waited with her future husband. Was she really going to marry him? She hurried to his side and said all the right words, her hand tucked in his. When the pastor announced it was time for Albert to kiss his bride, she could see on his face that he'd rather do anything than press his lips to hers. Nathan had always told her she was pretty. Had she somehow become hideous since his death?

He barely brushed his lips against hers before thanking the pastor and leading them all out to the wagon. Once they were there, she removed the money she had remaining from what he'd sent and pressed it into his hand. "We were careful and didn't use all your money. I want you to have what's left."

He looked at her in surprise, but simply nodded and put the money into his pocket. No other words were spoken between them during the hour long drive to the ranch. The children talked in the back. Several times she heard Clarence exclaim as he saw a cowboy ride past. She didn't turn around to see, but she was certain his face was lighting up as he talked about what he wanted to do when he grew up.

When they pulled up to the ranch, she could see that the vegetable garden hadn't been tended. She'd have to see to that next year. Hopefully he had enough supplies that she could make good meals for them all, because good cook that she was, without ingredients, they would still be hungry.

He helped her down from the wagon, and he and Clarence carried the trunk in. Clara walked into the house behind them, looking around her. The house was much grander than the one she'd lived in back in Massachusetts. The kitchen and parlor were two separate rooms. There was a bedroom downstairs that was obviously meant for her and Albert, and there were several upstairs.

The trunk was taken upstairs, and she was surprised by that. She pulled Albert off to one side. "The trunk has my things in it as well. Shouldn't we keep it downstairs?" She wasn't certain what he was thinking, but she'd been married before and she knew that intimacy was easier when you shared a bed especially when there were children around.

He shook his head, not meeting her eyes. "You'll be sharing a room with your daughter. At least for now." He walked back outside without saying another word to her.

She stood staring after him with surprise. He wasn't planning on sharing her bed with her? She shouldn't be surprised, she knew, and she certainly wasn't disappointed. She couldn't imagine sharing a bed with a man as prickly as her new husband.

She walked to the kitchen and looked at the stove, which was much fancier than any she'd ever used. The kitchen had a pump, and she was pleased to see that he had a good supply of food. Everything she would need was there, except fresh meat, and she was certain he'd provide that as he could. She was assumed he was a hunter, but she really had no way of knowing for certain.

The kitchen was dirty, and the floor was dirtier, but she could see he'd made an effort to keep things up. She knew how hard it was to play both mother and father to children, so she wouldn't say a word. She suspected that his ranch was in much better shape than his house, since that's what he was familiar with doing, not the cleaning and cooking.

She hurried to fix a simple meal out of the food he had ready for her. She found a loaf of bread, some eggs, and some milk and made some French toast. She didn't normally make breakfast for dinner, but she didn't normally cook a meal for six people after being on a train for a week either. If he didn't like it, he could cook his own meal.

The children were upstairs becoming acquainted with one another, and she could hear their voices drifting down the stairs as she hurriedly cooked for them all. She would have normally sent Clarence outside to help with the evening chores, but she knew he was just as tired as she was. None of them had slept well on the train, and with as long as the journey was, they were all ready to just sleep for a week. Tomorrow would be soon enough to get him started with learning to work the ranch.

She mentally made a list of things she'd need to accomplish the following day while she cooked. The children would need to be signed up for school. She would need to give the house a good thorough cleaning. She wished she could keep Natalie home with her to do that, but she couldn't let her daughter get behind in school. She needed to make an inventory of all the food so she could fix meals for the family. She also needed to go through all of the new family's clothes and see if anything needed to be mended or replaced.

She had enough fabric that she could make a few dresses for Gertrude, and some clothes for Robert as well. She just needed to find out what they were lacking. She wanted to make sure they had enough food for the winter set in within the next few days, because from what she'd read about the area, if she didn't have the food she needed in September, they may not make it through the long winter.

When she finished making the French toast, she called up the stairs to the children to come down to eat. Albert came in just as they were all sitting down. She'd poured milk for everyone, and the toast was in the center of the table with butter and syrup she'd found to be used for it.

Albert said a quick prayer and they all ate in silence. Her children, who usually never stopped talking, seemed in awe of their new step-father and afraid to speak in front of him.

Once dinner was finished, she stood to wash the dishes, but Albert stopped her. "Let the girls do the dishes. Gertie knows how to dry them, and I'm sure Natalie knows how to wash."

Clara collapsed back into her chair gratefully. She was willing to do the dishes if she needed to, but she certainly liked the idea of the girls doing them after each meal. She looked at her husband, wondering if she could talk to him without him getting angry. "Where's the school? I need to sign the children up tomorrow." She hoped they wouldn't be walking too far to the nearest schoolhouse.

He shook his head. "There's no school close enough for them to go to. Closest is in Billings, and that's an hour drive each way. Most folks around these parts teach their children at home."

Clara blinked a few times. "I've never even considered that. I have their school books, but I'm no teacher!"

He shrugged. "How hard can it be? Follow the books and give them lessons to study." He looked at Gertrude where she stood on a stool drying the dishes. "Time for Gertie to learn too. You can sit them all down together."

Clara sighed. Apparently she had no choice. She wished she'd known that before coming out here, but she'd make the best of it. Hopefully soon there'd be a school the children could attend. "I guess we'll get the house in shape and start school on Monday."

Albert nodded. "Sounds smart." He continued to watch the girls as they washed the dishes. "Both girls should be able to help you a lot around the house." He seemed to be looking for topics as well, wanting to get to know her, but feeling awkward about it.

"Yes, they can. Clarence would like to help around the ranch if you think he's old enough to do so. He's got in his head he wants to be a cowboy."

Albert smiled at Clarence, who was sitting there, hanging on their every word. "You want to go out to help me mend fences tomorrow?" He had a mare he could let the boy use. An eight year old could be of some help around a ranch. Not as much as a teenaged boy, but if he trained him right now, he'd be able to do a man's work in a few years.

Clara was surprised to see Albert smile. It was the first time since she'd met him that he hadn't looked stern. The smile completely transformed his face into something that could almost be called handsome. Maybe as he became more comfortable, he'd smile more.

Clarence nodded emphatically. "I would like that a lot, sir."

Albert made a face. "Sounds good."

"I'll work hard." Clarence looked down at the table as he said that, obviously embarrassed.

Albert looked back at Clara. "We'll eat at sunrise or a little before. I'll leave the girls and little Robert with you, and take Clarence. If he's a good help, he can come with me every day and learn in the evenings. It won't hurt him."

Clara bit her lip, but nodded. She could see the wisdom in his words. A boy who learned a trade young was so much more likely to have a good job as an adult. She was just thankful that Albert didn't think he needed to abandon his studies altogether. "That would be fine. Do you want me to teach Robert to read when I teach Gertrude?"

Albert seemed to think about it for a moment, but he shook his head. "No. Not yet. Gertie is eager to learn, but Robert still enjoys playing too much. Let him be a little boy for another year or two." He shrugged. "If he shows an interest, teach him his letters or numbers. Otherwise, let him play."

"That's what I'll do then." She looked at the four children and new husband she'd be taking care of. "Is there anything in particular you want me to cook for supper tomorrow?"

He shook his head. "I'll butcher a chicken in the morning, and you can do something with that if you would. I'm going to butcher one of the steer on Saturday so you can make some plans for beef for next week. Got some salt pork in the cellar, but never had any idea how to fix it. My Sally was good at those things, but I have no idea what I'm supposed to do when I get in a kitchen."

"That's why I'm here. I'll handle the meals." She looked over at Gertie. "Do you want me to start teaching Gertie how to cook and keep house right away? Or give her another year or two?" Some men thought girls should be able to just play with dolls until they were teenagers, and she didn't want to do anything that would offend him.

"My wife had already started her on those things, so more training will be good for her. Just teach her whatever you're working with Natalie on. They both need to learn to be good wives."

Clara looked at Gertie's dress, which was much too short. "I'll start making her dresses as well, if you'd like."

He gave a nod. "She needs new clothes."

When he didn't say anything else, she stood. "Clarence, I want you to wash up and head to bed. If you're going to be doing a man's work tomorrow, you'll need to get a good night's sleep." The boys were going to be sharing a room, so she looked down at little Robert as well. "You need to get ready for bed as well, Robert."

Robert stood and followed along meekly. "Call me when you're ready, and I'll come in and listen to your prayers," she told the boys. "I'm going to go upstairs and wash up as well. When you girls are finished with the dishes, come on up. We'll get ready for bed then."

She looked at Albert still sitting at the table and gave a quick nod. "Good night, Albert. I'll have breakfast ready first thing in the morning."

Albert sat at the table watching her walk away. She was a pretty woman and very pleasing on the eyes. He had done well choosing a new bride. He sighed and bowed his head. He didn't want to notice that she was pretty. It was his job to remain true to Sally. He loved her, and she'd given him two beautiful children. No, Clara was only there to cook, clean, and take care of the children. His needs came last.

Clara changed into her nightgown and climbed between the sheets of the bed she was going to share with Natalie. She bowed her head and whispered, "Please God, help me to do the right thing for this family. Albert is hurting. Gertie seems so sad. They all need a good woman to take care of them. Help me to be that good woman. I can't fail at this. I need strength."

Chapter 3

CLARA WOKE EARLY THE following morning, as was her habit. She hurried down to the kitchen to start breakfast, knowing that Albert wanted to make an early start of things. It had been a long time since she'd been able to stay inside all day and only do women's chores. She was glad she had this chance, and she was going to prove to everyone that this is what she was meant to do.

She went to the cellar through the hatch in the floor and brought back up some eggs, milk, and bacon. She'd toast the day old bread he'd gotten at the bakery, and they'd have scrambled eggs with bacon and toast for breakfast. While she was down in the cellar, she had seen some cream. They had a tiny bit of butter made up, and she'd see if she could get some butter churned today as well. The churn was sitting in the corner. It had cobwebs on it, but she could clean it up and use it for the purpose it was intended for.

Cooking on the fancy stove was a bit strange, but she quickly found her stride. By the time she heard footsteps overhead, she was scooping the scrambled eggs into two bowls, and she quickly buttered the last of the toast. She had found a jar of preserves in the cellar as well, and put them out with the rest of the meal. She had just finished pouring milk for the children and coffee for herself and Albert when he reached the bottom of the stairs.

"I woke the children and told them to dress and come down," he told her. He stood awkwardly for a moment, watching her work.

"Thank you. I was just about to go up and wake everyone." He was wearing a pair of work pants and a button up flannel shirt. She'd purchased some flannel and decided one of her first projects would be to make Clarence some flannel work shirts like Albert wore. She could already see the hero worship forming in her son's eyes, and she would do whatever she could to foster that and help it grow. A boy needed a man to look up to, and Clarence had been fatherless for too long.

The children rushed down the stairs one at a time. She was surprised to see how excited Robert and Gertie were when they saw the scrambled eggs. It was as if Christmas morning had come early. "Eggs!" Gertie squealed. "You made eggs!"

Clara nodded slowly. "Do you like eggs?" She couldn't tell if the child was upset that she was making eggs or happy about it.

"Oh, yes! I love eggs." She took her place at the table and immediately heaped a serving of eggs onto her plate before putting some on Robert's plate for him. She stared down at the eggs with a big smile while she waited impatiently for Albert to say the prayer.

Albert stared at his daughter with a half-smile on his face, shaking his head. "Stop being silly and bow your head so we can pray."

"Thank God for the eggs, Papa. Please!"

Albert sighed, and Clara looked between the three of them. She wasn't going to ask now, but she knew she could get Gertie to tell her what was happening later. She was a great deal more forthcoming than her father was.

After they finished eating, both girls immediately went to the sink to work on the dishes, and Clara was thankful Albert had started that the night before. It would be easy to always have the girls do the dishes now that he'd asked them to do them the first night.

Albert and Clarence left, headed for the barn to do the milking and gather eggs before they left to do their fence mending for the day. When they brought the eggs and milk in, she thanked them both. Clarence's chest was puffed up with pride that he was actually helping on a ranch even though he was doing the same work he'd done on their farm back home.

As soon as they headed out, Clara started a huge pot of beans soaking. She'd add a little bacon, and they'd have a filling meal of beans for lunch, and possibly for supper, because she was certain Albert had forgotten the chicken he'd promised her.

While the girls washed the dishes, Clara swept the floor, and knew she'd need to mop it before they could go on with their day. She hated to work in a dirty kitchen. She sent the girls upstairs to make the beds while she scrubbed the floor, and then they mixed the dough for some fresh loaves of bread together.

Clara had always enjoyed working in the kitchen with Natalie, and it wasn't until she worked with the much younger child, that she realized just how capable Natalie had become in the kitchen. She was proud of her daughter and her abilities.

Natalie went to get the cream while Clara and Gertie cleaned the butter churn. Natalie came up with the cream and Clara set the two girls to work churning the butter, Natalie's hands over Gertie's, while she formed the bread dough into dinner rolls. She thought everyone would enjoy having dinner rolls with their beans and fresh butter for lunch.

While they worked, she asked Gertie, "Why were you and Robert so excited to have eggs for breakfast?"

Gertie sighed heavily. "Papa can't cook. Anything. We went to town once a week to buy bread, and we had bread and jam for every single meal. I love jam, but not for every meal!"

Clara bit her lip to keep from snickering. The man had needed a wife a great deal more than he'd let on. She promised herself that she'd cook good meals for her new family, if only to make up for all the jam sandwiches they'd had in the past few months. "What's your favorite dessert?" she asked.

Gertie thought about that for a moment. "I really like gingerbread. Do you know how to make gingerbread?" Her face was hopeful as she looked at her new step-mother.

Clara smiled. "I'll look and see if we have the ingredients, and if we do, I'll make a big pan of gingerbread and some whipped cream for dessert tonight. Would you like that?"

"Oh yes!"

Natalie rolled her eyes. "I like pie, Mama." She made it clear that her needs still needed to be met as well.

Clara sighed, looking at her daughter. "You had pie on the train, Natalie. How long has it been since you've had gingerbread, Gertie?"

"Since before Christmas."

Natalie groaned. "I guess we're having gingerbread, aren't we?"

"You like gingerbread, Natalie. What's the problem?"

Natalie just shrugged her shoulders and continued to churn the butter. She didn't say anything else, but Clara could see something was bothering her. She'd have to talk to her about it when they were alone.

The three of them spent the day doing chores. They scrubbed walls, windows, and floors. They baked bread, and cooked the beans. Clara found the ingredients for gingerbread and carefully showed both girls how to make it, happy that she had another girl to teach. Clara had always wanted a houseful of children, and there just hadn't been any more after Clarence. She was happy to get two more from her new marriage.

She tried not to let herself think about Albert and his rejection of her the previous night. She didn't really want to sleep with her new husband yet anyway. She barely knew him, and the mere idea of having relations with another man felt as if she were betraying Nathan. She'd loved her husband with everything inside her, and she couldn't imagine letting another man take his place in her bed...or in her heart.

When Clarence and Albert came home for lunch, they seemed like they'd become closer during the day. Albert put his hand on Clarence's shoulder and told him what a good job he'd done that morning. After their prayer, she asked, "Was Clarence a good help?"

Albert nodded. "He held the wire in place so I could nail it in. It's been a hard job to do by myself all these years, and I'm glad to have another man around who can help me."

Clara smiled at her son, letting him know without words how proud she was of him. "Will he be going out with you again this afternoon?"

"He'll be going with me every afternoon. I need his help."

Clarence all but glowed with the pride the words filled him with. He ate more than she'd ever seen him eat in a single sitting, but he'd done a man's work, so that made sense to her.

"What's your favorite dessert?" she asked Albert as she ate her own food.

He eyed her for a moment, before finally answering, "Pie, but I don't need you to go out of your way to make it for me." He didn't really want her to do nice things like that for him. He wanted to be able to keep her at arms-length, and he couldn't really do that if she was constantly going out of her way to do nice things for him.

She grinned at Natalie. "That's Natalie's favorite as well. If I make it, both of you will enjoy it." She looked at Robert, who had played quietly all morning. "What's your favorite dessert, Robert?" She winked at her daughter, pleased to be making two people happy and not just one.

Robert shrugged. "I like them all. Cake, pie, gingerbread, muffins, and even candy!" He bounced in his chair as he said the words, making it clear that if it was sweet, and she made it, he would eat it.

Clara laughed. "Well, you'll be easy to please then!"

Albert reached over and ruffled his son's hair with a smile. "He'll eat just about anything you put in front of him. Especially now."

Clara didn't ask why especially now, because she understood. After the girls finished the lunch dishes she looked at the pot of beans and realized there were still more than enough for supper. Since she'd made dessert to go with it, she wouldn't worry about serving the same thing twice in one day.

"Let's go for a walk this afternoon," she suggested. She was hoping there would be some fruits they could pick on the ranch or something she could use to spice up her cooking.

The girls readily agreed. They'd done a lot of what needed to be done that day, and she was happy to give them a rest. Robert skipped along behind them, happy he didn't have to nap.

They found some apple trees, and she looked at the apples on the ground, but they were all full of worms and decayed. "It may be too late in the year for us to pick apples," she said with a sigh.

"The apples up in the tree still look okay, Mama," Natalie protested. "Do you want me to climb it and get some?"

Clara thought about it for a moment, and back home, she'd have agreed in a heartbeat. Here they were just too far from a doctor if one of them fell. "I don't think so." She looked at it carefully, thinking about it. She could almost reach the lowest apples. "I know! Robert, do you want to get on my shoulders and pick apples? You can drop them to Gertie. Natalie, I'll need you behind me, helping to make sure he doesn't fall."

Robert nodded, his hair flopping with the movement. "I'm going to have to cut your hair soon," she told him absently. It looked as if it hadn't been cut in six months, and when she thought about when his mother had died, she realized she was probably right. Albert needed a good sheering too.

She picked him up and settled him onto her shoulders, allowing him to kneel there. His weight wasn't enough that it bothered her, but it gave him enough of a boost that he could reach at least some of the apples. Clara held him by his thighs, while Natalie stood behind her mother with her hands against his bottom, to keep him from falling.

He giggled over and over, obviously enjoying being up so high and picking the apples. He would drop one, and Gertie would catch it. She made a pouch out of the front of her skirt to carry them all in. When her skirt was filled, she said, "That's all I can carry."

Clara looked down at the amount they'd gotten and made a face. It was probably enough for two pies, but not many more. "Does your papa have a ladder in the barn?" she asked.

Gertie nodded. "He does. We could come back tomorrow with the ladder and pick a lot more!"

Clara smiled. "We'll do just that." She carefully lowered Robert to the ground. Walking to Gertie, she made a pouch out of her apron, and had the girls pass the apples to her. She didn't want Gertie to be burdened with the weight of them on the way home.

They continued walking, going back a different way, and found some fresh berries. "We'll come back and pick those after supper tonight. We'll bring some buckets. We'll make fresh jam, applesauce, and lots of pie filling for the winter."

The children were obviously happy that she was thinking forward to the sweets they'd want to eat when winter came. They hurried back to the house and she found an empty barrel for the apples. It had apparently once held flour, but it would work for now.

During dinner that evening, she brought up her plan of picking berries that evening and apples the following day. Albert shook his head. "We'll get the apples tonight while Clarence and I can help, and tomorrow you four can get the berries. It doesn't make sense for you to be climbing on a ladder when Clarence and I can do it tonight."

So they soaked the dinner dishes instead of washing them right away, wanting to save on daylight. The six of them carried three burlap bags and a ladder to the apple tree, and Albert held the ladder while Clarence climbed it. They were able to fill all three bags with apples. Clara was delighted. "This will make our winter so much tastier!"

On the way back, she spotted some wild pumpkin in the dim light of the setting sun. There were only three of them, so she took one that she carried under one arm while she carried a burlap bag over the other. Both Gertie and Robert were given the job of carrying a pumpkin as well.

By the time they reached the house, they all had sore arms. Clara followed Albert into the barn as he put the ladder away. "The girls are tired. They've worked all day. I'm going to let them go to bed, and I'll see to the dishes myself."

Albert shook his head. "No. They need to know that no matter how tired you are, you don't go to bed without finishing all of your responsibilities."

She wanted to argue with him, but she knew he was right. The children did need to learn to be more responsible. "All right." She hated asking the girls to do it, but she would, because she wanted to raise the best girls she could.

They walked up to the house and saw that the girls already had the job half done. There were bags full of apples leaning against the walls in the kitchen while the pumpkins sat on the floor. She had a lot of work ahead of her to get everything canned before it went bad, and she knew she wasn't going to pass up the chance for berries the next day. Blackberries had always been her favorite, and she was going to have lots of blackberry pies through the winter. The patch had been a big one, and she was going to take full advantage. It was a good way to teach the girls to work while the sun shined as well.

It was obvious to her that Albert felt very strongly about instilling a strong work ethic in all four of their children, and with that as his philosophy, she was going to make sure she worked hard to do the same with them.

Her new husband may not want to be married to her, but she knew that he would be a good father to her children, and a good provider for them all, so she couldn't complain. He seemed to be a good man, but he was very obviously still a sad one over the death of his first wife.

She still missed Nathan every day, but she'd had two years of back-breaking work to distance herself from his horrible death. He'd been out working the fields one day and hadn't come home. She'd found him there on the ground. The doctor had said his heart had just given out. He'd been such a young man, it had seemed ridiculous to her that he could die that way, but she couldn't argue.

After she got the children to bed, she went back down the stairs, wondering if Albert would be willing to talk to her. She did miss adult conversation a great deal. She poured herself a glass of milk, and sat at the table across from him. "Is there anything in particular you want me to do first? Around the house I mean?"

He gave her a blank look and shrugged. "I don't even know what needs to be done. I tried to keep everything up, but I've never kept house in my life. I've never cooked a meal that didn't end up in the trash either."

"You've done a good job with the house. Better than I did with the farm I tried to run." She smiled at him to let him know she understood. "I'm planning on going out and picking the berries with the children in the morning. Then we'll spend the next couple of days canning everything to have it ready for the winter." She didn't know why she was explaining it to him when he obviously didn't care, but she needed to talk to someone. "Do you know if there are other vegetables or fruits that would be ripe about now that I could can for the winter?"

He shrugged again. "My wife did all that."

"Okay." She asked something she'd been worried about for a while. "Do you think we could head into town and buy more supplies before the snows start? I'm worried we'll be stuck here."

"I'll make another trip into town at the end of this week or beginning of next. If you'll make me a list of what you need, I'll take Clarence, and we'll get enough for the winter. Usually, we can get through on the sleigh, but I can't make any promises. Some winters are worse than others."

She nodded. "I'll make the list. I'd like more food and some fabric so I can make the girls some more clothes. Both need a couple more." She looked down at her dress. "This is the only work dress I have that isn't old and patched over and over. I need to make some more for me as well. Clarence needs shirts. I'm sure Robert does also. Sewing is a good way for me to keep the girls occupied in the winter. They need to be able to keep their hands busy, so their minds won't be idle."

"Just write it all down, and I'll take care of it."

"I have some money from selling my things before I left Massachusetts. I'll give it to you before you go."

He shook his head. "I don't need your money. I make more than enough to support this family. Save it for when Natalie marries, and she needs things to set up a household." He hated the idea of using the money she'd made before coming there. If they were destitute, he wouldn't hesitate, but he made good money, and there was just no need.

Clara nodded, not liking his answer, but agreeing to do as he said. "I'll do that then." She stood up, taking her glass to the sink and rinsing it out. "Good night."

He seemed lost in thought as she left the room, and she didn't feel his eyes watching her as she climbed the stairs.

Albert sighed as soon as she was out of sight. He rested his elbows on the table and put his face in his hands. He'd never dreamed that having a woman around the house would wake up the old desires in him. He'd truly thought he was immune and would never feel passion again without Sally. Now here was this new wife of his, working hard for his family, and doing it so prettily.

He liked that she worked so hard, but why couldn't she have a wart on the end of her nose, or be unattractive in some other way? How was he going to be able to resist her forever? He needed to be able to help his children remember his wife forever. Why was it that it was so hard to remember Sally when Clara was in the room?

SHE STUMBLED INTO THE kitchen at the same time as he did the following morning. He started the fire in the stove for her, while she ground the coffee beans. She rubbed her hands over her arms, trying to warm them. "Would you like anything special for breakfast?" she asked.

"No, just something to fill my stomach. Anything will do." He hated that she was such a good cook. Sally had tried, but she'd never enjoyed cooking, and had been unable to come up with creative ways to fix food. He hated comparing the two women, but couldn't stop himself. "I'll get the eggs and milk." He left without another word.

Clara stared after him, wondering what she'd done wrong. She felt like she constantly fell short of what he wanted from her. She wished she knew how to make him happy, but with the way things were going, she was certain he'd never be happy with anything she did.

She stirred the batter for pancakes and had just taken the first of them off the griddle when she heard footsteps behind her. The children were up, and the boys took their seats at the table waiting for their meal. The girls automatically set the table for her, and they poured the last of the milk from the previous night into the cups for everyone.

When Albert came back into the house, the table was set and everything was ready. He looked at the pile of pancakes on the plate she'd set in the center of the table as well as the bacon. "Looks good," he said, complimenting her efforts for the first time.

She smiled. "Thank you." Taking her seat at the opposite end of the table from him, she bowed her head and waited while he prayed. It was her third day there, and she felt like she'd done nothing to break the ice that had formed between them. How could she spend the rest of her life with a man who only wanted a cook, maid, and nurse for his children? She needed so much more than that.

While the girls did the breakfast dishes, she made the beds. She hadn't been in Albert's room before, and saw that he had a photograph of a young woman on his dresser. She assumed it was his first wife, Sally.

Sally was very different physically from Clara. She had blond hair and her eyes looked light, although it was hard to tell from a photograph.

She made his bed quickly and picked up his dirty clothes from the corner of his room. She and the girls would spend some time doing the laundry before going out and picking berries. She looked at the bed she'd already made, and with a sigh, stripped it clean. The sheets and quilts needed to be washed as well. It wasn't something she'd planned for the day, but she'd do what needed to be done.

She was coming out of his room with the linens in her arms when he walked into the house with a chicken. She took it from him and plucked the feathers, scalding it and preparing it for supper. They'd have something simple for lunch, probably bacon sandwiches, and she'd make a big pot of chicken and dumplings for dinner.

The girls started on the laundry while she prepared the chicken for boiling. Natalie efficiently showed Gertie the correct way to use the scrub board and how to rinse everything perfectly clean. Clara felt the pride prick her again that her daughter was so adept at doing household tasks and so willing to help her younger sister. The girls got along well, despite the four year age difference. She couldn't be prouder of the girl she'd raised.

Each of the children carried two pails to put the berries in, and she took along a huge cook pot. She wanted to get as many of the berries as they could before they went bad or animals got them. The four of them worked quickly and efficiently, leaving not a single berry on the bush for scavengers.

They carried their bounty back to the house, and Clara began the painstaking process of washing the berries and removing the twigs that inevitably ended up in the mix. She lost track of time, and it was just before noon, when she realized that she hadn't fixed lunch. "Natalie, hurry downstairs and get the bacon from the cellar. I'll heat up the frying pan. We're having bacon sandwiches for lunch."

Without being told, Gertie quickly set the table and got everything as ready as she could. When Natalie gave the slab of bacon to Clara, she rushed over to start slicing the bread while Clara sliced off pieces of the bacon to fry.

They weren't quite finished when the men came in, and Clara apologized. "I was caught up in getting the berries ready for canning and lost track of time. I'm so sorry."

Albert looked disappointed, but he said nothing. They all ate quickly, and he and Clarence hurried out to finish their day together. Clara hoped he wasn't angry with her.

She worked with the two girls, laughing at the sight of Gertie standing on a chair that had been turned backwards with an apron wrapped around her so she could be of some help. Robert took a nap in his room, because he'd started rubbing his eyes and become cranky.

By the time the men came in for dinner, the chicken and dumplings were cooling on the corner of the stove, and they had filled every jar in the house with homemade preserves and pie filling. She still needed to take care of the apples and the pumpkins, but they would keep longer.

The bread from the previous day was still good, but she toasted it, buttering it before she put it into the oven to make it a little tastier. The girls had helped her make two pies for dessert, so she knew the majority of her family would be happy with the treat.

She hadn't been able to get the clothes in from the line yet, but she'd do that while the girls did dishes after supper and get everything folded and put away. After the prayer, she looked at Albert. "I'm going to need several more jars to be able to finish the canning. I haven't done the apples or the pumpkins yet."

"I'll see to that Friday. Can it wait that long?" Albert looked up from his meal long enough to ask.

"Yes, that would be wonderful. Would you also see if anyone is selling any other fresh fruits or vegetables? I'd love to have some green beans, carrots, potatoes… anything you can find really. I'll can what I can and a lot of that will just keep in the cellar through the winter."

He shrugged. "I'll get whatever anyone is selling. A lot of times farmers will try to sell fresh produce on the side of the road leading into Billings. If I find that, I'll buy some of everything and let you do what you want." He looked down at his meal and grunted. "You did a fine job on dinner tonight."

She smiled, knowing it took a lot for him to be able to give a compliment like that. "Thank you. I'm sorry lunch wasn't ready when you got here."

He shrugged. "No matter. We got a lot done today anyway. I'm amazed at how much faster work goes with my helper." Life was easier all around with his new wife and her children. He hated to admit it, because it felt like a betrayal of Sally, but Clara was a much better housewife than his first wife had ever been.

Clarence flushed with pleasure, and Clara smiled happily. As hard as it was for Albert to compliment her, it seemed to come naturally for him to compliment the children. She knew it meant a lot to her son to hear that he was doing well. "I'll make that list tonight and tomorrow. I do want to make sure we have enough to make it through the winter if we get snowed in."

Albert nodded. "We'll do fine." He'd been in Montana long enough that he respected the winters, but he didn't fear them. He hoped his wife would calm down in her fear of them soon.

Clara looked at the girls. "I'm going to get fabric for you each to have some new clothes as well. If you want to think about colors, you can let me know." She looked at Robert. "Do you want to pick the color for your new shirts?"

Robert shrugged. "Whatever Papa likes."

She smiled, having expected that answer. She was almost excited for the canning to be over so she could move on to making the new clothes for her family. She'd never been fond of sewing, but after spending two years farming, she was thrilled to have the opportunity to stay in and do women's work.

After supper, Albert and Clarence went out to do the milking while the girls dealt with the dishes. Clara went to the line and took everything down. She was happy the quilts were done, and she wouldn't have to wash them again until spring. She carried everything in, carefully folded the clothes, and went in to make each of the beds.

She did the children's first, because they went to bed before the adults, and then she went downstairs to fix Albert's bed. She was spreading his quilt over his sheet when he came into the room. She flushed, feeling like she was intruding when she was in his bedroom. He stood watching her for a moment, obviously not pleased to find her there, before turning from the room.

She followed him out, sitting at the table with him. "I'm sorry to be in your space that way, but your bedding needed to be washed." She wondered how to get him to look at her when she talked to him. Why did he dislike her so much?

He gave a brief nod but didn't respond any other way. He hated seeing her in the room he'd shared with his wife. Why did if feel like such a betrayal?

She sighed. "Why didn't you just send off for a maid and a cook instead of a wife? You don't have any desire for a wife."

He shrugged. "Wouldn't have been proper for one thing. And I'd have had to pay a maid. Wife works for free." He knew his words sounded cold, but they were true. He really didn't have the money to pay a woman to do the things a wife would do for free. He wasn't poor, but he wasn't rich either.

She shook her head sadly. "I'd have taken on the job of a free maid if it meant my children would have food, clothes, and a roof over their heads."

He shrugged again, not willing to pursue the topic.

"Will I ever be more to you than the woman who cooks and cleans and cares for your children?" she asked, her voice obviously annoyed. She was glad the children were in bed instead of hearing this conversation.

He sighed. "I don't really know. I like you fine. That's not it at all. I just...I lost my wife eight months ago. I'm not ready to let someone take her place yet." He couldn't believe he was telling a beautiful woman he wouldn't take her to his bed, even though she was his wife. Was he even a man any longer?

"I see." She felt the tears prick her eyes as she rose from the table. She wasn't sure why it mattered to her that he didn't want to be married to her, but it did. "I'll get you that list tomorrow."

"Clara?" he called.

She turned, surprised to hear her name on his lips. It was the first time he'd said it. "Yes?"

"You're doing a fine job with my children. I appreciate the meals and all the hard work. We're going to be fine. I just need time." He hated hurting her, and he knew he had. Just because he wasn't over his first wife, didn't mean he had to treat his second wife poorly.

She nodded, turning back around to climb the stairs up to the bed she shared with Natalie. She hoped he was right and they would be fine. She didn't want to feel lost for the rest of her life.

Chapter 4

CLARA KEPT WORKING hard for her family. She finished the canning with the supplies he brought from town and helped him with curing the meat from the steer he'd butchered. They both knew it would need to be used as quickly as they could, but he said he'd do another as soon as the snows started. Once they would remain frozen they'd stay better longer. She was simply happy to know they'd have food through the long winter. The main thing that had concerned her about moving so far from the city was the winters.

The fall cleaning was done, and the first snows blew through. She started the children on schoolwork and patiently taught Gertie to read. Robert listened in as much as he could, and he learned his letters and the sounds he made, although she didn't push him to learn. Natalie was self-sufficient in her schoolwork, and usually finished within a few hours each day.

They were falling into a good schedule, and Clara was pleased. Every day she'd sew on their clothes while they did their schoolwork, and every evening after they went to bed, she'd work on gifts she was making for them for Christmas. She decided to make sweaters for both girls and scarves and stocking caps to wear under their cowboy hats for all three of her men. Robert would love being included with the other two.

She and Albert would talk quietly while they worked, getting to know one another. He talked about what it was like to grow up in Texas, and how much he'd loved his Sally. She'd talk about growing up in Massachusetts and about Nathan. They talked about when the babies were little and how much they loved them. One thing they never mentioned was their future together. Clara found the omission sad.

As the nights got longer and the days got shorter, they found themselves having more and more time together in the evenings. There was really no work that could be done on the ranch after dark, so they'd come in earlier at night. One night, while they were sitting around the table with the supper dishes put away, Gertie asked Albert to play his guitar.

Clara looked at him in surprise. "You play guitar? I've never even noticed one."

He shrugged. "I keep it under the bed and out of sight. I haven't played in a year."

Clara did some quick math. He hadn't played since his wife had fallen ill then. "Please, play something for us," she asked.

He shook his head. "I don't know that I can." He had loved playing for Sally, but now that she was gone, he just didn't feel like playing any longer. How could he?

Clara didn't ask again. Instead, she had the children play together, not meeting his eyes. While they were awake, she was working on a new dress for Gertie. She stabbed the fabric a little harder than she needed to, pushing her needle through. Some day he would consider her good enough to be married to. She looked at Albert. They'd been married a month and a half, and the only time he'd even kissed her was when he was forced to by the pastor.

Clara studied him as she worked. He was carefully whittling a piece of wood, for what purpose she had no idea. She wondered what it would be like to kiss him, for real, and not just because they were sealing their vows.

She finished the hem on the dress and called to Gertie. "Let's go upstairs and try this on. I want to make sure I don't need to change it at all."

Gertie was practically bouncing with excitement over the pretty dress.

"Use my bedroom," Albert called.

Clara bit back a retort that it was all his bedroom was good for. She sighed to herself. Why did it make her so angry that he wouldn't treat her like a woman? It wasn't like she was in love with him!

No, she didn't love him, but she was interested in learning if love was even an option between them. She wanted to get to know the man better, and possibly have a real relationship with him. She felt like he owed her that chance. He should be courting her and treating her like she was someone he cared about, instead of ignoring her so much.

She helped Gertie into the dress and smiled when it fit so well. She'd left plenty of room in the waist for it to be taken out so it would fit for longer and had left room at the hem for it to be taken down. The dress should fit for at least a couple of years to come.

Gertie insisted on wearing it into the big room so the family could see it on her. Albert told her she was almost as beautiful as her mother, and Gertie sat on his lap and hugged him.

Clara had known there was great affection between father and daughter, but had never before seen the two of them display it with her sitting on his lap. She'd never heard him mention her mother to her before either. She felt as if she was completely left out of the situation, and it made her sad.

As she helped Gertie get out of the dress, she sighed. She needed to have a talk with Albert. They'd been married long enough that she should be able to tell him how she was feeling. Shouldn't she?

Once the children were tucked into bed that evening, Clara returned to the table and took out her crocheting. The girls' sweaters were coming along beautifully. She took a deep breath and steeled herself before saying, "Is there something wrong with me?"

His head jerked up from whatever he was carving. "What?" He was married to a beautiful, capable woman who seemed able to do just about anything, and she thought something was wrong with her?

"I want to know if there is something so ugly about me that you find you can't look at me or treat me like anything other than a maid.

I've been married to you for six weeks and the only time you've ever kissed me is when the pastor told you to. The only time you've ever touched me is to help me get in and out of the wagon. It's not natural for us to be married and never touch or kiss." She didn't look at him as she said the words, and instead she concentrated on the hook in her hand as it formed the small sweater.

He sighed. "There's nothing wrong with you. I actually think you're very attractive." He set the wood and knife in his hands onto the table and braced his hands on his knees. He looked at her as he said the words, hoping she'd understand. "I loved my wife more than I've ever loved anyone. When she died, I felt like a part of me died too."

Clara's eyes met his, and she shook her head. "You act like you think I don't understand losing someone you love. I loved my husband something fierce, but it doesn't feel right to me to tie myself to you for life, and not at least explore whether or not we could have feelings for each other. I could love you, even though I loved him. Just like I love your children, even though I love mine." She looked down again. "I just know what we're doing isn't right. We made vows to each other, and we're ignoring those vows."

Albert shook his head. "I'm not ignoring them. I'm postponing them...for now. I need a little more time."

"How much?" she asked. She wasn't sure what was prompting her to push him this way, but she just didn't feel right about the way things were between them.

His Adam's apple bobbed as he stared at her. "How much?"

"How much time do you need? A week? A month? A year? A decade?" She met his eyes again, feeling stronger than she had in a long time. "How much time do you need before you can stop thinking of me as someone you hired and start exploring the fact that you now have a wife?"

He let out a breath. "I don't know. How long do you think I should need?" His voice was more than a little irritated with her. Why was she pushing him? Usually the man was the aggressor, and he'd never dreamed he'd be married to a woman who would be demanding her rights.

She shrugged. "I don't know. I just need to know that there's a possibility between us. The way things are just doesn't seem right."

He sighed. "No, they don't to me either. I just don't feel like I have anything left to offer a woman." How could he? He'd buried his heart in the grave with his wife.

Clara put down the sweater and her yarn and walked around the table, taking the seat beside his and pulling it close. She put her hand on his arm. "You have so much to offer. I watch the way you are with the children and know there's a loving caring man inside you. You treat my children just like you treat your own. The love is there. Why can't you just give me a chance?" Even Clara couldn't believe the words that were coming out of her mouth. Why she was practically begging the man for his love. Did she have no shame?

He looked at the hand on his arm, and then he looked up at her. His tongue moved out to wet his lips. He'd wanted to kiss her for weeks, but felt like it would be a betrayal to Sally. Could he kiss her...and be a husband to her, without feeling guilty? Would it be wrong to move on? If it was just physical, and he didn't let his emotions get involved, would that make it all right?

He scooted his chair a little closer to hers and cupped her chin in his hand. "I know it seems strange to you, but I feel odd touching any woman but my wife this way."

Clara's eyes were a warm brown in the light of the lantern. "Your former wife you mean. I'm your wife now."

He nodded, and his gaze dropped to her mouth. He'd noticed her full lips before, and wondered how it would feel to kiss them for real. Slowly he lowered his head toward hers, half afraid of what would happen when their lips actually touched.

Clara watched as his mouth descended toward hers, her eyes finally closing as his lips brushed against her own. She felt a shudder of surprise as he kissed her. There was an electricity between them she hadn't felt with Nathan. She parted her lips for his kiss, and he immediately swept his tongue in to deepen the pressure. His hand left her jaw and moved around to the back of her neck, holding her mouth in place for him.

Her hands crept up and moved to his shoulders, caressing them softly while her lips returned his kisses. She'd missed being intimate with a man. She'd missed kissing and being held. Her husband's death had shut down that part of her nature for a long while, but now? Now she was ready for more, and she was married to this man.

After a long moment, Albert pulled his head away staring down at her with surprise. "I'm not sure we should have done that," he said to her.

Clara shook her head. "I'm sure we should have. Albert, I know how you feel about your late wife. I do. But we're not buried with our first spouses. We're here, and we need to go on for ourselves and for our children."

He stared down into her eyes for a moment before sitting up straight and staring off over her shoulder. "Let's leave things as they are for another week or so. I'll try to be more...affectionate during that time. I'll touch you more. Kiss you more. We'll see how we feel in a week, and if we both want to, maybe you can move your things down to my bedroom." He almost choked on the words, hating the idea of sharing the room he'd shared with Sally with any other woman, but knowing that she was right, and the way things were between them was unnatural.

She nodded slowly, standing up. She was a lot more shaken by his kiss than she'd thought she'd be. It wasn't like she was a young virgin who had never been kissed. She'd been married for nine years. "That sounds fine." She stood and gathered up her crocheting and hid them away again. "Good night, Albert."

He was blocking the way to the stairs. "I said I'd be more affectionate." He put his arms around her and tenderly kissed her good night. "Good night, Clara." He walked to his bedroom and shut the door with a snap.

Clara took the lantern and used it to guide her to her bed. As she undressed in the darkness and put her nightgown on, she knew that things would never be the same between them again. No matter what happened from here, they could never go back to the easy friendship they'd had the past few weeks.

She slipped into bed beside Natalie, and she knew she didn't want that easy friendship back. She needed to see how things would work out between them. She needed to know that they could have a real marriage.

THINGS DID CHANGE BETWEEN them after that night. He kissed her good morning when he saw her each morning before the children rose. After the children were in bed, the two of them would spend time together, sitting close. Sometimes they would kiss, and sometimes they would just talk, but always they'd be touching somewhere, even if it was just their knees through the layers of clothing they both wore.

As they got closer to their self-imposed deadline of one week, Clara got more and more nervous. Would he reject her, or would he invite her to share his bed? She was nervous at the idea of sharing a bed with a man she'd known for such a short period, but she'd put herself in this situation, and she truly didn't want out of it.

Albert thought of her during the day while he worked. He found himself daydreaming about what it would be like to lay Clara bare on his bed, and press between her spread thighs. He wanted her. There was no doubt about that, and if he didn't give her his heart, there was nothing wrong with having relations with her, was there?

On the day they'd given themselves as a deadline, he'd sent Clarence on to the house after milking with the promise that he'd be in shortly. He'd gone to kneel at Sally's grave, right there on the other side of the road from the barn. He explained everything to her. "I know it must seem to you as if I'm cheating on you, but I'm not. I still love you. I never would have remarried so soon if I hadn't needed a wife so badly. It was for the sake of the children. Now, I find that the wife isn't happy to stay upstairs, but after two months, who can blame her? Please don't hate me, Sally. I don't love her. I could never love another woman the way I loved you. I'll just do my duty toward her, and that will have to be enough."

He stood and walked toward the house, wishing he could send the children to bed right away so he could take his wife to his bed. He wanted her. Badly. He could admit that to himself. He was ready to have a woman in his bed again. It had been over a year since he'd had relations. It was time. He was a man after all, and he had a right to make love to the new wife he'd taken.

Clara was more aware of her new husband that evening than ever before. Their kisses and discussions after the children had gone to bed for the past week had her waiting nervously to see how he would react to her. When he came into the house, he stopped at the stove where she was cooking to brush a soft kiss across her cheek. Her eyes met his in surprise, because he'd never done that in front of the children before. Did that mean he was ready to make their marriage a real one?

Clara took her seat at the table and listened to Albert's deep voice pray. She barely picked at her food, so nervous she was shaking. She had no idea what the evening would bring, but she was glad she would finally have an answer to some of her questions. She needed that answer.

The girls played with Robert after the dishes were done, slowly rolling a ball back and forth between them. Clarence sat at the table with her and Albert doing his arithmetic and asking questions whenever he had one.

Clara worked steadily on the new shirt she was making for Robert, taking her time with each tiny buttonhole. The painstakingly slow work made her concentrate on something other than what would be happening once the children were in bed.

Finally it was nine, and time for the children to sleep. She went up the stairs with them to see them to their beds as she always did. She'd left a nightgown hidden downstairs earlier in the day, just in case. She didn't know if she'd need it, but if she did, she wanted to be prepared. While Robert had napped earlier, she'd taken a bath in the big tin tub in Albert's bedroom as well. She wanted to be clean for him.

Robert wanted an extra story that evening, so she let all the children pile onto the bed he shared with Clarence, and she told one of her favorite bedtime tales from her childhood. Even though Natalie and Clarence had heard the story over and over, they enjoyed their time lounging on the bed, listening to the stories she told.

Finally, she got all four children into bed and crept silently down the stairs, looking at Albert as he sat at the table, whittling as usual. She took a deep breath as she walked toward him, waiting for his decision. She stopped just a foot in front of him, and he set his wood and knife down, taking her hand in his and leading her to his bedroom. He closed the door behind them, and he stood looking at her in the light of the lantern that he'd lit while she was upstairs.

His hands reached out to cup her face, and his eyes bored into hers. "I want you," he whispered softly. He wouldn't lie and tell her he loved her, but did that matter? They were married and raising four children together. They had a right to enjoy the benefits of marriage.

She took the big step between them that pressed her body against his. "I want you, too." When she'd first talked to him about all this, she hadn't really wanted him. She'd just felt like their relationship was strange and needed this, but after two weeks of kissing after the children went to bed and talking about everything under the sun, she knew she was ready to take the relationship to the next level.

He slowly lowered his head to kiss her. Her tongue darted out to wet her lips. He brushed his lips softly across hers as if savoring her feel. She moved her hands to his shoulders, silently urging him to deepen the kiss. Instead he quietly brushed her lips before standing straight and looking down at her again. "You're a beautiful woman."

She blinked a few times. He'd never complimented her on her appearance. Only on the things she did as a wife and mother. "Thank you," she whispered.

He didn't say anything else, just looked at her. She wondered if he'd ever get around to making love to her, or if he was going to take all night. On one hand, she loved the idea of a slow sensual feast, of kissing and caressing and making love all night long. On the other hand, she knew the next day would be full of responsibilities. What was losing one night of sleep for pleasure and getting to know her husband though? She could handle that.

"Sit on the bed," he urged.

She gave him a surprised look, but sat at the foot of the bed and watched as he knelt at her feet and carefully removed each of her shoes and socks. When he finished, he rubbed her feet for her, his hands sliding all the way up to her knees as they massaged her calves and the soles of her feet.

She sighed contentedly. "That feels so good."

The look he gave her gave nothing away. His were half closed, and she couldn't see his eyes at all.

She braced her hands behind her and leaned back against them, giving herself over to the feeling of having someone touch her intimately again after so long. Somehow even his touch on her legs made her quake with wanting him.

When he stood again, she shivered in reaction. The man certainly knew his way around a bedroom in a way Nathan never had. He took her hand and pulled her to her feet, unbuttoning the front of her dress. His lips brushed hers again as he pushed her dress off her shoulders and quickly divested her of her petticoat. He wanted to see her. She'd been his wife for over a month and he'd never seen her body. She'd been right. It was unnatural for them to be man and wife and parent together, but not make love or share a bed.

When she stood bare in front of him, his eyes traveled over her, noting the small marks at her waist indicating she'd carried children. Her breasts were full, and despite childbirth, her waist was small. He wondered why she'd never married again after Nathan had died. She was truly a beauty, and he wondered how he'd been fortunate enough to claim her as his.

Clara watched him as he looked down at her, wondering what was going through his mind. His first wife, Sally, had been beautiful, and she knew she'd never compare to her. She only hoped that seeing her this way wouldn't make him decide he was no longer willing to perform his marital duties.

Albert swept her close, kissing her face and neck and shoulders. He was no longer being so gentle and tender as he kissed her everywhere he could reach, alternately nipping at her skin and sucking the small bites. She wrapped her arms around him and rubbed his back through the layers of clothes he still wore. She wondered how he'd feel if she undressed him, and decided it didn't matter. She was his wife, and it was her privilege to undress him if she wanted to.

"You sit down, now," she whispered, trying to keep the embarrassment from her voice. She'd never been so forward with a man before, but she wanted to get him unclothed, and she wanted to be able to touch him while she undressed him.

Albert moved to the foot of the bed, and leaned back on his hands, taking the exact pose she had. She pulled until his cowboy boots came off, and then she ran her hand up inside his pants leg to catch the top of his sock and pull it off. She certainly didn't need to put both hands up there to remove his sock, but the look on his face told her he appreciated the gesture.

When she repeated the same action for his other sock, he watched her carefully wondering what his new wife would do next. She skipped the foot rub, and instead, got to her feet, and he was almost disappointed. He'd never had a naked woman kneeling at his feet before, and he'd enjoyed it.

She took his hand, helping him to his feet. As soon as he stood before her, she unbuttoned his long-sleeved flannel shirt and untucked it from his pants, pushing it to the floor. Under it he wore a plain white undershirt, and she pulled it over his head.

She ran her fingertips over the fine dusting of hair on his chest and down to the waistband of his pants. Her fingers danced over the front placket, and instead of unbuttoning him, she gripped him through his pants instead.

He let out a low groan. "Unbutton them," he whispered. "Take them off me and touch me."

She smiled up at him, stepping into his arms and brushing her bare breasts against him instead. He'd made her wait a long time for this night, and she wasn't going to let it happen too quickly. If he could tease her, then she could certainly tease him.

He gripped her bottom, cupping her close to him and forcing her into his hardness. His mouth dropped to hers and kissed her passionately, insistently. "I need you."

She smiled, her hands reaching down between them to unbutton his pants. "Do you now?"

He growled as her hands worked. "You can go faster than that!"

She laughed softly. "But why should I? I thought you liked things slow." She spread the opening in his pants wide, her hand moving beneath his underwear to grip his manhood.

"Yes, touch me there!"

She moved her hand over him, stroking him from base to tip and back again. "Like this?"

His hands gripped her shoulders as his knees went weak. "I think it's time to move this to the bed," he whispered.

She pushed his pants down over his hips and to the floor. "You think?"

He pushed her backward until she fell onto the foot of the bed, and then lifted her hips to fit her there completely. He stretched out beside her, his hand immediately going between her thighs while his mouth angled toward one breast, pulling her nipple into his mouth.

She arched against him, loving his touch on her. His hands were rough from the hard work he did, and his touch reminded her of what a strong man she was now married to.

He lifted his head, looking down into her eyes by the light of the lantern still burning on the dresser. "Are you ready for me?"

She nodded, nervous now that the time had actually come to join with him. She knew he'd be careful with her, but still, she'd only ever been with one man in her life, and it was odd to give another person this much...power over her body.

He rolled atop her and between her spread thighs, his eyes staring into hers as he reached down and guided himself inside her.

Her eyes fluttered closed as he pushed deep. She was startled at the pain she felt, but it had been so long for her, she knew she shouldn't be surprised. Her hands went up to grip his shoulders, and she clung tightly, waiting for the pain to pass.

Albert felt Clara tense against him and guessed that she needed a little time. He rested his forehead against hers, panting to get control.

After a moment, she pulled his mouth down to hers for a kiss, lifting her hips to invite him to continue. She stroked his back and shoulders, enjoying the feel of a man in her arms and inside her body again. It had been too long.

With all the constant touching of the past two weeks, she felt herself growing tense and readying much faster than she'd expected. As soon as she'd clenched around him, he finished, collapsing on top of her.

She sighed, kissing his cheek and holding him close. She'd missed the closeness of sharing her body with another person more than she'd missed the actual intimacy of sex. When he rolled to his side, she rolled with him, her head settling against his shoulder. She could think of nothing to say to him in those moments, and instead just stroked his chest with her hand while she lay close to him.

Albert held her close, his hand stroking her hair. He'd missed this part of marriage more than he'd realized. He had worried he would feel guilty over making love to a woman other than his Sally, but instead, he felt cleansed.

They fell asleep in each other's arms, both of them wishing they had the right words to say to the other. Maybe they'd find them tomorrow.

Chapter 5

CLARA WOKE WITH A START the following morning. The lantern was still burning beside the bed as she realized she was lying close to her husband with her legs tangled with his. She quickly rolled away from him, not wanting to meet his eyes. She couldn't believe how she'd acted the night before, teasing him as she had. He was her husband and should have been the aggressor in their lovemaking, not her.

She quickly pulled the nightgown she'd hid in his room over her head and rushed up the stairs to dress for the day. She washed herself quickly in the cold water from the pitcher in Natalie's room before changing into a clean dress and apron. She fashioned a bun on her head, and rushed down the stairs to start breakfast before anyone woke.

Albert was just coming out of his room when she reached the bottom of the stairs, and she found she couldn't meet his eyes. "Good morning," she mumbled as she hurried to the stove to start the fire.

He watched her scurry to the stove and wondered what her problem was. He'd thought their night had gone better than he could have hoped and had really expected most of the nervousness between them to be over. He pulled on his coat and headed to the barn to milk the cow and gather eggs, still contemplating what was going on with his new wife.

Did she regret coming to my bed last night? Did I hurt her? I know I did at first, but I thought she found her pleasure. Maybe I scared her somehow. He hurried through his chores, so he could run into the house and talk to her about the night they'd had. He wanted to be able to speak to her before the children came down.

When he got back into the house, he saw that Clarence was sitting at the table dressed for work, and Natalie was at the stove helping her mother cook. Natalie took him a cup of coffee while Clara quickly fried up the potatoes that were left from supper the night before. He loved that his new wife never wasted a thing. She worked hard to be sure they used all of their resources to the best of her ability.

Just the other night he'd watched her and the girls cutting up some of the old woolen dresses they wore. When he'd questioned it, Clara had explained they would braid the strips they'd cut into rugs so they wouldn't have to stand on the cold floor during the winter. Clara liked to be barefoot, and she would put one in front of the work table so she could work barefoot all through the year.

He took the pail of milk and basket of eggs he carried to the work table, leaning down to kiss her cheek as he set the things down. "You all right this morning?" he asked softly.

She nodded without meeting his eyes. She put the potatoes she'd chopped into the frying pan and broke several eggs into it as well. "Breakfast is just about ready. Sit down and drink your coffee."

He eyed her for a moment before walking to the table and the coffee Natalie had set at his place for him. He took a deep sip and sighed. He wanted to talk to her but knew that wouldn't be possible until the children were in bed.

All through breakfast, he kept watching her wondering what he'd done wrong. He certainly hadn't forced her into intimacy.

Clara felt his eyes on her through breakfast, and she felt as if she were the worst person alive. How could she have been so forward? Husband or not, he was the man, and he should have been the one to initiate things between them. She didn't know if he'd want her to sleep with him again, or if he'd send her back upstairs to stay with Natalie.

She ate her breakfast slowly, hoping he would leave with Clarence and not try to talk to her at all. She really didn't think she could face him.

Finally, he stood, thanked her for breakfast and set his hat on his head. "We need to move the cattle today, Clarence. You remember how I showed you to use your rope?" he asked. He couldn't waste more time in the house waiting for her to talk to him. He had to get some work done.

Clara watched the two of them leave the house, thankful again for how good he was with Clarence. She loved that he was teaching his son the skills that Clarence wanted to learn.

She spent the day as she spent every day, but she worried more than usual. By the time he came in at the end of the day, she'd decided she wouldn't wait for him to send her up to sleep with Natalie. She'd just do it herself. She'd go downstairs and talk to him as if nothing had happened after the children were in bed, and when it was bedtime, she'd simply climb the stairs and sleep with her daughter like she always did.

She wished she felt like she could talk to Albert about her concerns, but he had made it clear that he didn't enjoy talking about things like that, and she wasn't going to press him.

After she'd tucked the children in, she climbed down the stairs and saw him sitting at the table whittling as he did every night. "Would you like another piece of pie?" she asked.

He looked up, his eyes meeting hers. "That would be nice." He watched her as she moved to the stove and uncovered the blackberry pie she'd made for him. "It was the best pie you've made." He wished he had the right words that would make her stop being so prickly.

"Thank you." She cut two generous pieces and poured two glasses of milk, returning to the table to sit with him while they ate the treat.

He took a bite and sighed happily. "I've never met a woman who could bake quite as well as you do." He was almost ashamed to say it, though, because he had loved his first wife, despite her lack of cooking and baking skills.

She smiled, her eyes meeting his for the first time all day. "I bet you say that to all the ladies."

He laughed softly. "I don't think I've ever said it to anyone before." He looked down at his pie, wondering how to phrase his question. Finally, he decided he'd just say it. "What did I do wrong last night?"

She looked at him in surprise. "Wrong? You didn't do anything wrong. Why would you ask that?" She was shocked he would even bring up their night together.

He shrugged. "Well, I thought everything was fine between us, but when we got up, you weren't really speaking to me." What was he supposed to think about that?

She sighed, staring down at her pie and flicking at the crust with her fork. "I just feel like I shouldn't have pushed you into intimacy. That's the man's place, not the woman's."

He blinked in surprise. "If you hadn't pushed me, we'd have waited a lot longer to be comfortable with each other. I think you were right. The way we were together was unnatural."

"But I still shouldn't have done it, and I'm sorry."

He shook his head. "You should have done it. You did the right thing for both of us." Albert stood and took his empty pie plate to the basin for her to wash with the breakfast dishes, going back to the table and removing her empty plate to set next to his. "But if it makes you feel better, tonight I'll be the one to start things off."

He took her hand and pulled her into the bedroom, shutting the door with a snap behind them. He pulled her into his arms and kissed her soundly. As soon as her mouth was free, she looked up at him. "You really don't mind?"

"Mind? I can't think of a man alive who would mind. I enjoy making love with my wife."

She smiled, her head resting against his shoulder. "Then I guess we're all right?"

He laughed softly. "We're more than all right."

THEY FOUND AN EASY routine after that. Their first real challenge was the first blizzard to roll through. As soon as Albert realized how bad it was, he strung some rope from the house to the barn so he could go back and forth easily to milk the cow and collect the eggs. They'd known a storm like this was bound to come, but she'd been surprised to see the first so early in the year. It was only early November. She was pleased that he wouldn't allow Clarence to go out to the barn with him in the bitter cold.

Clara had planned on washing clothes the morning of the blizzard, so she simply strung a line up in the cellar and dried the clothes down there, keeping to her routine as much as possible. Natalie, Clarence, and Gertie sat at the table working on their schoolwork, while Clara mended clothes. Robert played quietly as he did every day while the older children completed their studies.

Albert was the problem. He paced the room. Back and forth. Back and forth. He couldn't be still. "Are you all right?" Clara asked when she got too dizzy to let him continue.

He nodded once and resumed pacing. Clara tried again. "Do you want me to get your whittling for you?"

He shook his head, continuing to pace. She assumed it was just that he didn't enjoy being stuck indoors, so she kept up her work, and tried not to notice his pacing. After the children were in bed, and all the work for the day was finished, he finally explained. "Every time we have a blizzard, we lose cattle. I always worry we'll lose too much of the herd to keep going."

Clara's eyes widened with understanding. "When will we know how they fared?"

"When the blizzard is over. Hopefully this one will just last a day. Sometimes they're four or five."

They'd had blizzards in Massachusetts, of course, but they hadn't had cattle to worry about. Farmers weren't affected as much by the blizzards as the ranchers. She tried not to worry.

Finally after the third day, the winds died down, and he and Clarence left to assess the damage. They only lost a few head. He was relieved as he told her of their losses in bed that night. "I've lost as many as a hundred head in these storms. We were lucky this time. Only five were lost."

They were thankful there weren't more lost during the storm. "I'm so glad. Five isn't good, but it could have been so much worse."

"I know." He hugged her close.

"For Christmas I'd like to have a turkey. Do you think you could get one? I want to make stuffing and mashed potatoes and gravy. I know my kids love that."

Albert nodded in the darkness. "I can do that. You have big plans for Christmas?" Sally had always made a big production at Christmas time, and he loved the idea of continuing that for the children.

"I'd like our first Christmas together to be special. I've made special gifts for all the children. I still need to finish Clarence's, but the others are done."

"And what would you like for Christmas?" he asked.

"Oh, I don't need a gift. I have everything I could possibly need."

"So you're going to rob the children of the joy of giving you a gift?" he asked in mock surprise.

"I just don't need anything."

He sighed. "We'll think of something."

THE ONLY THING THAT kept Clara from being completely happy during the first months of her marriage was not understanding her husband. He would be kind and considerate at times, but he was sullen and withdrawn at others. She could never understand what would happen to turn him moody.

One evening in mid-December while they were eating supper, he announced he had to go into town the following day. She'd written two letters: one for her parents and one for Elizabeth Miller to let them know she was faring well. She wrote to Elizabeth because she wanted to, but to her parents, because she felt obligated.

"Would you post some letters for me while you're in town?" she asked. She really wanted to go with him. Would he be angry if she asked?

He gave a curt nod. "Have them ready in the morning."

"I've already written them. I was just waiting for you to go to town to mail them." She looked at the children. "Would it be all right if we all went with you?" She clenched her hands together in her lap, hoping he'd agree.

He looked at her in surprise. "Well, I don't know about that. It will be very cold."

She shrugged. "We have coats, and we'll cover up with quilts. We can take some hot potatoes for our lunch, and they'll keep our feet warm." If Albert and Clarence could handle the cold, then she and the others could too.

He studied her for a moment before finally saying, "I suppose that's fine. Make sure the children are dressed for it, though. I don't want any complaints about how cold it is."

"I won't complain," she said with a smile. She looked around at the children. "Will you complain if it's too cold on our way to town tomorrow?"

They all shook their heads. "We want to go!" Gertie said, in a way that told Clara that a trip to town was a big treat for his children.

Back in Massachusetts her children had walked to town every day to go to school, so it was a bit odd to her that his children went to town so rarely.

The next morning dawned with a bitter wind, but she was determined to take the children. She put long underwear on all of them, and then put their regular clothes over the top. They all wore coats as well. She took every quilt in the house in an effort to keep them warm. She'd gotten up well before dawn so she could bake some potatoes for their lunches, which they would also use to keep their feet warm.

After breakfast Albert turned to her with a look of worry. "Are you sure it's not too cold for the children?"

Clara nodded. "The children will be fine." The sleigh had two seats and the three older children sat in the back together while Robert squeezed between Albert and Clara on the front.

The ride to Billings was very cold, and they all huddled together, but the potatoes kept their feet warm, and Clara was happy to get out of the house for a while. She wanted to try to find just the right knife for his whittling. It was his only hobby, and she wanted him to have something special to do his carvings with. She still had a bit of money from the sales of her household goods in Massachusetts, so she could afford one.

Of course, they also needed more flannels and more yarn so she could continue making clothes that would keep them warm through the winter. She had even begun working on a new quilt for Robert with all of their old ragged clothing they no longer would wear.

It was really too cold to talk much, so they sat huddled together under the blanket that covered them. When they reached town, he helped her down from the sleigh while the children found their way down. They all went into the mercantile to look for different things.

It was the first time Clara had been to the store in Billings, so she wandered around for a moment to figure out where everything was. She went to the fabric table, and saw that the knives were directly next to the bolts of cloth. She fingered some of the materials while she looked over at the knife display. There was one that had a man on a horse with a cowboy hat and a lariat, and she smiled. That was the one she wanted.

She chose six different colors of flannel for new underclothes for everyone as well as new nightgowns and dresses. She quickly chose some yarns and some dried goods, but there wasn't much they needed in the way of food. Her husband had obviously planned on being snowed in for the winter and chosen accordingly.

She took her purchases to the front and explained that Albert would be paying but said she wanted the knife for him for a Christmas gift. She wanted that wrapped and given to her alone. She got the amount and gave him the money she had in her pocket. "Thank you for your help," she whispered.

She went over to the pot display and looked at what they had. There were a couple of huge pots that she would love to have to cook with, but she wasn't going to ask for anything for herself. As long as he was seen to and the children had whatever they needed, she was content.

While she was looking, she overheard a conversation. "Look at her standing there acting as if she has a right to spend his money, when he paid for her to come out here and marry him." It was a low feminine voice, and Clara bristled at its tone.

Another voice reached her. "I can't believe someone would actually become a mail order bride. You'd have to feel like you were bought and paid for. It must be like being a slave."

Clara felt tears pop into her eyes and walked across the store to a small display of pocket watches. She wasn't going to let the women hurt her feelings. She'd put up with a lot of snide remarks back in Beckham when she didn't immediately remarry and instead tried to make a go of farming. She could handle this.

ALBERT LOOKED AT THE display of brooches on the table in front of him. He knew that Clara had sold her favorite cameo brooch before leaving Beckham so she wouldn't come to him with her children in worn clothes. She hadn't told him, but Clarence had told him a lot while they'd worked together. He was glad he had the older boy to divulge things to him.

As he looked over the display, a couple of local ranchers came up beside him. "You sure do have all the luck, Hanson."

Albert looked at the other man, Frank, wondering what he was talking about. "Why?"

"You had the prettiest wife in town, and when she died, you send off for a mail order bride. You could have gotten some ugly thing with a terrible personality, and instead, you end up with a pretty little bride who actually seems to enjoy being here. How do you do it?"

Albert knew the other man was referring to how many of the local rancher's wives seemed to go crazy during the long winters. He shrugged. "You're right. I'm lucky." He didn't talk about the anguish he'd felt when Sally died. These men were idiots, and he would never share anything personal with them.

The second man, John, shook his head. "Maybe I'll send off for a mail order bride too. If I can get one as pretty as yours, I'll start looking forward to going to bed at night."

Albert wasn't going to listen any longer. "Do you two actually need something?"

The first man shrugged. "Nothing more than a little bit of your luck."

Albert chose the brooch that he thought looked as much as possible like the one Clarence had described. He picked it up, and kept his hand clenched around it while going toward the front.

The second man followed along with him. "I guess that means you care for the pretty new wife. Sure got over the other fast, didn't you?"

Albert said nothing as he paid for the purchases that had been stacked on the long counter for them. He knew that Clara had added some things, and he'd told Clarence to pick something out for Clara from him.

Samuel, the merchant, put everything into wooden crates for him. "Nice new wife you have there, Albert. Glad to see you're not always having to come to town for bread any longer."

Albert nodded before making his first trip out to the sleigh with their purchases. He put it on the floor at the back of the sleigh knowing the children would be able to deal with less leg room better than he and Clara could. Clarence showed up right behind him with a crate to put in as well. The look on his face gave Albert pause.

"What's wrong, Clarence?" Albert had never seen the boy anything but jovial. Had someone said something to him as well?

Clarence shrugged. "Nothing."

"I know something's wrong. Tell me what it is."

"A man in the store asked me if you were my pa. I didn't know how to answer that."

Albert smiled, happy it was something so simple. He put his arm around the boy's shoulders and led him back into the store to get the girls and little Robert who he'd set Natalie to minding. Clara didn't get to shop enough, and he knew women liked to buy new things. "I'm your pa. As soon as your ma married me, I became your pa. I don't care what other people say or think."

Clarence's eyes brightened. "Can I start to call you 'Pa' then?"

Albert nodded. It was only then that he realized the boy had never called him 'Pa' but he didn't call him 'Albert' either. He was always just called 'sir.' He should have realized there was a problem months ago. "I'd be honored if you called me 'Pa.'"

After they'd carried the last of their purchases to the sleigh, Albert went back inside to get Clara. "Time to go." As soon as he looked at her, he couldn't help but think about what the ranchers in the store had said. Had he really replaced Sally too quickly? Yes, his children needed good food, but he could have managed a bit longer. Couldn't he?

He helped Clara and Robert into the sleigh before climbing up beside Robert. "Do you want to eat before we leave or stop on the way?"

Clara was fighting back the tears from what the women had said. She'd needed to be strong in their presence, but now she needed to be alone so she could cry for a moment. She didn't want to show weakness before her husband or children. "I'd like to get out of town first. Even go all the way home. It's not that late."

Albert looked at her for a moment before clicking to the horses. She was upset, just as he was. They needed to stay out of town and away from people who would upset them.

He drove straight to the house. While he and Clarence unloaded the sleigh, Clara started a fire while the girls got Robert out of his winter gear and set the table. She took the now cold potatoes and put them in the oven for a few minutes to warm them while she set out butter to go with them. She poured milk for the children and heated up the coffee from the morning for herself and Albert.

While they ate, Albert kept looking at her as if he were just realizing she didn't belong in his house. Clara could barely control the tears. She knew she needed to wait until the girls were doing the dishes to cry, but she wasn't certain she could hold out that long. She couldn't let the children see her cry.

Albert watched Clara while they ate, wondering what had been said to hurt her so much at the store. Why couldn't people just accept that they'd done what they needed to do and let two lonely people find happiness together?

Clara escaped to her room soon after lunch. Albert and Clarence had gone onto the range to take more hay to the cows, Robert was napping, and the girls were washing dishes. She lay down on the bed for a moment and cried her eyes out. She knew she wasn't as pretty as his first wife. She knew that every time she spotted the other woman's photograph, which was still on the dresser. She was doing her best to be a good wife and mother, though. Did that count for nothing?

She took ten minutes wallowing in her anguish, and then realized there was nothing she could do but work harder and try to please him more. She knew he enjoyed their time alone together while the children were in bed at night. That was something. Eventually maybe he'd have some affection for her. Right now, affection seemed to be too much to ask.

She hurried into the main room, still feeling chilled from her time in the sleigh. She made a thick stew for supper filled with carrots and potatoes and some of their own beef.

By the time Albert got into the house, she was in a surly mood, angered that he hadn't known anything was wrong. The table was set and they were ready to eat. Everyone ate in silence, her anger filling the air, and he seemed to be angry as well. She had no idea what was wrong with him, though. What did he have to be angry about? She did everything for him and his children.

After tucking the children into bed, she walked down the stairs, thinking she'd just get her nightgown and sleep upstairs with Natalie. She didn't have much of a desire to be around her husband. She certainly had no desire to sleep beside him through the night.

When he saw her go into their bedroom, he stood and followed. "What are you doing?"

"Getting my nightgown. I'm going to sleep in Natalie's room with her tonight."

"What is your problem? When we left town, you seemed upset and now you seem angry enough to hurt someone. Why?" The look on his face told her he didn't want to put up with her mood.

She brushed past him without answering. He grabbed her arm. "What have I done to make you so angry?"

She spun on him, wanting to lash out at him for everything that had been said about her in town. Everything that had ever been said about her or her children. For every time she felt inadequate. She knew she was being unfair, though, and tears sprang to her eyes again. "Nothing."

"You're angry with me for no reason then?"

She nodded, walking up to him and burying her face against his chest, relieved when his arms folded around her. "I can't explain it. I'm never this emotional!"

He held her close, rocking her in his arms. "It's a hard life here."

She nodded, knowing that wasn't it either. She would love her life there if she wasn't so unsure of him. "I just wish I didn't always feel so inferior."

He pulled away from her, staring at her in shock. "Inferior? You really feel inferior? Why?"

She shrugged. "I feel like I don't cook well enough. Like I don't sew well enough. I'm not a good enough mother. Your children deserve their real mother, who did things the way she did them. They shouldn't have to put up with me."

He shook his head in disbelief. "You are a wonderful cook. There's never anything left when you cook. How could you not think that you're good enough?" He sighed. "Robert barely remembers his mother at all. She was sick for most of his life, and the doctors couldn't figure out what was wrong. Even when she was well, she wasn't the kind of cook and mother you are. You have everything perfect around the house all the time. She never did."

Clara stared at him. "I never have anything perfect. I have two girls who work beside me all day to make the house as presentable as it is!"

"I guess we all see our own shortcomings. I don't see you as having any. I think you're a fabulous wife and mother."

She bit her lip against the words she truly wanted to say. She wanted to ask why he didn't love her if she was a good wife and mother, but she knew that was completely inappropriate. He was still mourning Sally. She walked to the dresser and put her nightgown on top of it, knowing she'd wear it that night. Walking back into the main room, she got her crochet hook and yarn and sat at the table. "Tell me about Sally. How did you meet her?"

He sat down with his whittling, a new block of wood in his hands. "We were neighbors growing up. We both lived in a small Texas town. It was my dream to be a rancher, so I saved up every dime I could, and remained living at home with my parents until I had enough to buy a small piece of land and some cattle. My father was the barber in our town, and I was an only child." He carefully made a long slice through the wood. "Sally waited for me. She was five years younger than me, but I was thirty before I felt like I was ready to marry and start our lives together. We married on her twenty-fifth birthday."

Clara was startled a woman would wait for a man so long. That never happened in the east that she'd seen. "Did you move up here right away?"

He nodded. "We got married and started our journey the next day. We got our land here, and our cattle, and began our lives together. She was happy here for the first few years. We had Gertie three years after we married and then Robert. She was so sickly after Robert was born. I kept begging her to go to the doctor in town, but she kept saying that it was just that she needed time to recover from childbirth. By the time we got her to the doctor, he said it was too late. If I'd taken her sooner, he might have been able to do something, but I didn't."

Clara squeezed his hand. "You can't blame yourself for her death."

"I can't not blame myself for her death. She was a good woman, and I loved her, and I let her die." He shook his head, his eyes dark and sad. "How did your husband die?"

"He had a heart attack while working one day. Finances had been tight, and the doctor said he just worried himself to death."

"And you tried to farm after his death?"

She nodded. "I couldn't see remarrying so quickly, although I had a couple of offers. When the bank told me they were foreclosing, I felt like I had to get out of town. I had to figure out a way to raise my children without the constant worry that I was feeling."

"And you answered my letter. I'm glad you did."

"You are?" She was truly astonished by that fact. She thought he resented her.

He nodded. "You're a good wife to me and a good mother for my children. How could I not be glad it was you who came to marry me?"

She was pleased by his statement but not sure if she really believed him. He'd obviously truly loved his wife. She would always be second best.

Chapter 6

IT WAS LATE THE FOLLOWING afternoon, when she'd just sat down after baking six fresh loaves of bread and a cake, and had dinner in the oven staying warm for when Albert and Clarence got back that she heard a knock on the door. In the months she'd been there, they'd never had a visitor.

Clara jumped to her feet and rushed to the door. She blinked twice at the woman in front of her. She was a carbon copy of Sally. She knew because she'd looked at the other woman's photo enough, hoping she could be more like her.

"May I help you?" she asked softly.

"I'm Mary. My brother-in-law lives here. At least I think he does. Is this Albert Hanson's house?" Mary acted as if she had every right in the world to be there, and Clara had no thought of turning her away.

Clara nodded. "Yes, of course it is. Come in."

Mary waved to the driver of the sleigh, and he drove off. It was only then that she realized Mary had a carpet bag. "Thank goodness. I thought I was lost." The pretty woman in front of her had blond hair and green eyes. Her cheeks were rosy from the cold. She picked up her bag and hurried into the house, warming herself in front of the fire. "My husband died last month, so I came here to keep house for Albert. Where is my brother-in-law anyway?"

Clara was stunned to hear the question. Did she not know Albert at all? "It's the middle of the day. He's out on the range working."

Mary nodded. "Okay. Well, where's my room?"

Clara studied the older woman, trying to figure out what to do with her. "Well, we really don't have any empty rooms." Her gaze settled on the girls sitting at the table doing their schoolwork. "Would you two be willing to share so Aunt Mary can have a room to herself?"

Natalie and Gertie exchanged looks. "Yes, ma'am," they said in unison.

Clara smiled, happy that was resolved. "Okay, girls, run upstairs and move all Gertie's things into Natalie's room." She looked at Mary. "I'll change the sheets in Gertie's room when they're done." She walked to the stove and started the coffee pot. "Are you hungry? I made a cake that's still cooling." She'd planned to serve it for supper, but she could whip up a pie while she waited for the coffee to heat up.

Mary shook her head. "Oh, no. I don't eat cake. I'm watching my figure."

Clara smiled, looking at how slender Mary was. What was she going to do with her? "I understand." She sat at the table. "Have a seat. I'm Clara by the way. Albert and I married in September."

"Oh. I had no idea Albert had already remarried." Mary frowned. "I guess he doesn't need a housekeeper after all." The look on her face told Clara she was very upset that Albert had married without first discussing things with her.

"You can stay with us for a while. We have plenty of room." Clara hoped the other woman would be gone as soon as possible though. She didn't want to have to feel like she was in the shadow of her husband's late wife for the rest of her life. She already felt that way a great deal of the time. Having someone who looked just like her in her home would only make things worse.

"Oh, wonderful! I'll help however I can around the house. I can see you're having a hard time of it." She walked to a window sill and wiped her finger along it as if to say Clara's home wasn't clean enough.

Clara bristled. Everything in her home was kept just the way she wanted it to be, and she spent hours scrubbing every day. "That will be nice. I'm sure there are some special dishes you know how to make that you could teach me." She'd be as polite as she could be during the other woman's time there. Maybe Albert knew of a single man they could marry her off to. Quickly.

"I'm sure I do. Albert loved my sister's cooking. I could teach you to make everything she used to make for him."

Clara smiled, knowing the other woman wouldn't realize how strained the smile was. "Thank you. I'd like that."

Robert came down the stairs then, rubbing his eyes from sleep. He looked at Mary for a moment before hurrying into Clara's arms. He was obviously nervous around the stranger. "How long has it been since you've seen the children?" Clara asked as she held Robert in her lap.

"Oh, I've never seen the children. I haven't seen Albert since the day he married my sister." Mary walked over to sit across from Clara. "I'm your Aunt Mary," she said to Robert, trying to take him from Clara's arms.

Robert looked at her out of the corner of his eye, obviously wanting to stay where he was. "He's shy when he first wakes up," Clara explained quickly. She didn't know if that was true or not, but she didn't want the other woman's feelings to be hurt that he wouldn't go to her.

"Nonsense. He wants to be held by his Auntie Mary, don't you, boy?"

Boy? Didn't she know his name? "Robert, Aunt Mary would like to hold you."

Robert shook his head and buried his face in the crook of Clara's neck. "I want you, Mama."

Clara shrugged. "I'm not going to force him."

"Why not? You're spoiling my nephew. Sally would hate that!"

"Sally's not here to hate it." Clara cuddled the boy close, knowing he was upset by the argument going on around him. What was wrong with Mary to upset her nephew this way? She hoped that Albert told the woman to leave. She didn't think he would, but she could always hope.

Clara pulled dinner out of the oven and set it on the table. She made gravy with the drippings in the bottom of the roast pan and then set the table. The girls were still moving rooms, so she couldn't ask them. She was surprised that Mary, with all her talk to being a housekeeper for the family, didn't get up and do it, but she seemed content to watch Clara work.

Albert stepped into the house, stomping on the rug just inside the door, taking off his coat and hanging his hat on the peg by the door. He moved out of the way while Clarence did the same. He walked straight to Clara and leaned down to kiss her. "Dinner smells wonderful."

Clara smiled up at him, pleased the first thing he did with Mary there was show her affection. "We have a guest," she said, using her thumb to indicate the table. Robert usually sat at the table while she finished preparing a meal, but instead, he was clinging to her skirts.

Albert reached down to lift his son into his arms before turning to the table. He did a double take. "Mary?" he asked, his voice obviously shocked. He didn't move over to her, but instead stood with Robert right beside Clara. "What are you doing here?"

Mary walked across the room and pulled Albert down into a hug, squeezing Robert in the process. "My husband died, so I had to decide what to do. I thought with Sally gone, you could use a housekeeper." She looked at Clara with a disgusted look. "Looks like you've already replaced her though."

Clara froze with surprise. *Did Mary really just say that to Albert? What is wrong with that woman?*

Albert's voice was stiff. "I found a new wife. When Sally was dying, she told me that she didn't want me to spend the rest of my life alone." His gaze met his sister-in-law's evenly.

"You could have waited a respectable amount of time."

"I'm through discussing this, Mary. Why are you here, and how long will you stay?"

"I came to help you. I already told you that. I don't know how long I'll stay. I actually hoped that things might work out between us..."

"You can stay as long as you're not a burden. You'll help Clara with chores and do your part. As soon as you stop, I'll put you on a train straight back to Texas." Robert obviously felt no love for the woman, despite her resemblance to his first wife.

Clara breathed a sigh of relief. Maybe she wouldn't stay for long after all.

"What would I do in Texas? Mama and Papa are gone."

Albert shrugged. "I'm sorry about the death of your family. I have some friends in the area who are looking for a wife." Albert thought of the two men from the mercantile the day before. He'd love to see one of them marry his sister-in-law. All they cared about was getting a pretty wife. Mary was pretty all right.

"You wouldn't mind seeing me married to one of your friends?"

He shrugged. "Honestly, I don't care what you do as long as you don't cause problems in my house."

He walked to the table and sat down, still holding Robert. "What did you do today?" he asked the boy.

Robert shrugged. "I had breakfast and lunch, and I practiced writing my letters and counted a lot. Mama made me take a nap again." He made a face.

Albert smiled, hugging the boy close. "Mama was right to make you nap. You have to nap everyday if you want to grow up to be a big strong cowboy."

"And eat all my supper!"

"Yes, you need to eat all your supper." Albert saw Clara was pouring the gravy into a bowl. "Let's wash our hands so we can eat."

Clarence was still standing in the doorway, holding his hat in his hands. He was obviously uncomfortable about the situation. Albert noticed him standing there and he smiled. "Wash your hands, boy. Your mama has supper almost ready."

Clarence nodded. "Yes, sir." He rushed to the basin and washed his hands as soon as Albert and Robert were through. He took his normal seat at the table, even though it was beside the stranger.

Mary smiled at him. "I'm your new aunt, Mary."

"Hello." He said nothing else.

Clara put the dishes on the table. "Clarence? Would you run upstairs and tell your sisters that it's supper time, and they can come down? They can finish their task after supper."

Albert leaned against the sink, looking at Clara. "What do you have them doing?" he asked.

"They're moving all of Gertie's things into Natalie's room. Natalie's room is bigger, and the girls can share it, while Mary takes Gertie's room."

Albert shook his head, not liking the situation. Mary had once pulled the wool over his eyes, and he wasn't her biggest fan, but he couldn't see tossing her out on her bottom like he wanted to do. He had loved his wife too much to treat her sister that way. "That's fine." He put Robert into the seat beside him, knowing that the young boy didn't want anything to do with his aunt. He took his place at the head of the table, and figured everyone else could take care of themselves.

Clara put all the dishes of food onto the table and then took her seat at the foot. The children came barreling down the stairs a moment later, and they all looked at the stranger. "I didn't think. There's an extra chair in our room." Clara stood to get the chair. "Excuse me."

Albert shook his head. "I'll get the chair. You start serving the children."

Robert usually sat beside Clara so she could fix his plate easier. With him down on the other end of the table, it would be harder. She stood and walked down to him, fixing his plate. "Do you want more carrots?" she asked.

Robert nodded. "I love carrots!"

"And they're good for you. I'm glad you like them." She finished fixing his plate and hurried back to her place just as Albert came back with the chair. He placed it beside Clara at the table and Natalie slipped into the seat, because Mary was in her normal place.

After Albert prayed, while they passed the food around, Clara told the children, "This is Aunt Mary. She's going to be staying here for a while." She pointed to each of the children as she said their names. "That's Robert, Gertie and Natalie, and Clarence is sitting next to you."

Mary smiled sweetly. "I'm sure we're all going to get along just great."

All of the children watched her warily while they ate, and there was no real conversation. "Did you girls get most of Gertie's things moved?" Clara asked.

Natalie nodded. "We had just finished when Clarence came up to get us."

"Oh, good. I'll go up and change the linens on Gertie's bed while you girls do the dishes," Clara said.

Albert shook his head. "If Mary's going to be staying here, then she needs to do it herself. She can't expect you to wait on her, Clara."

Clara sighed. "I was just thinking it would be okay for tonight, because she obviously traveled a long way."

"I *am* very weary from my travels," Mary interjected.

"Mary needs to do it herself," Albert repeated. "When Clara first arrived she'd been on a train with two children for a full week, and she came home and started cleaning and cooked supper without a single complaint. I expect you to do your share."

He said nothing else until Mary said, "I'll do it, Albert."

As soon as supper was over, Mary disappeared upstairs with her carpet bag and the sheets Clara gave her. Clara sat down beside Albert while Clarence started to work on his schoolwork. "I'm sorry if I shouldn't have invited her to stay," Clara said.

Albert shook his head. "No, I won't turn her out." He sighed heavily. "Mary was Sally's twin. I courted her, and she ran off to marry someone else, because I wasn't ready to settle down yet. She had no children. I married Sally, because as soon as Mary left, I realized she was the one I'd loved all along." He pulled Robert into his lap again. "I guess Mary decided that since both of our spouses were deceased, we should get married. I never encouraged her to think that. I don't really want her here."

Clara bit her lip. "But you courted her once, and she looks exactly like your first wife. Don't you wish you'd waited to marry her?"

Albert shook his head. "No, I really don't." Nothing else was said about the matter, because Mary came back down the stairs.

Clara hurried over to get the dress she was hemming for Gertie and spread it out on her lap. Her fingers picked up her sewing where she'd left it off the night before. Each of the girls would have new dresses for Christmas, and the boys would have new suits. She'd been working hard on them, and wanted them to wear them to Christmas morning services. They weren't able to go to church often, because of how far out they lived, but she really wanted to attend service on Christmas, and Albert had agreed.

Albert picked up his whittling, and the girls finished the dishes before settling down with their crocheting. Both girls were trying to make some fine lace for pillow cases for their hope chests.

Mary plopped down in a chair with nothing in her hands, and once again tried to entice Robert to come to her. Instead, he sat at the floor at Clara's feet, playing with a small wooden train his father had made for him. "Robert, I look just like your mama did. Come play with me."

Albert looked at Mary. "We use the time after supper to work quietly, because Clarence is doing his schoolwork. He's out on the range with me all day and needs to keep up his book learning."

Mary sighed heavily, but didn't say anything else. Instead she leaned back in her chair and looked around the room. After a moment, Clara asked, "Would you like to use some yarn and my crochet hook? My knitting needles? You're welcome to work on something quietly yourself." She couldn't imagine how it would be to sit completely idle with nothing to do.

Mary shook her head. "Oh, I don't do those things." She sighed. "I prefer to talk to the people around me and get to know them."

"We have plenty of time for that during the day after the girls finish their schoolwork," Clara said with a smile, bending back to her task.

They worked silently for two hours with Mary just looking around her. By the time they were finished, Clara was ready to kick the other woman. She didn't want her girls to think that idleness was okay.

Finally, Clara stood, the dress hemmed. "We'll try that on you in the morning, Gertie. I think it's going to look beautiful."

Gertie smiled. "Thanks, Mama. I can't wait."

"Time for bed, everyone." Clara watched as Clarence closed his book and returned all of his schoolbooks to their place on the bookshelf in the corner of the room. Both girls gathered up their crocheting and put them into the work basket Clara kept. Robert stood and started climbing the stairs. Clara followed closely behind Robert, hoping that Mary would take the hint and go to bed as well. She didn't want the other woman there during her quiet time with her husband.

She met with the children in the boys' room as always. She told them one bedtime story, and tucked each of them into bed. Natalie had always joked that she was too old to be tucked, but Clara found the girl still loved the individual time it got her with her mother.

Once all the lights were off upstairs, Clara started down the stairs, knowing Mary had stayed down with Albert. "I can't believe you married *her*. She couldn't look less like Sally. What were you thinking?"

"I marry who I want to marry, and you have no say over anything I do. You gave up those rights. I'm glad you're finally meeting the children after all these years, but I'm not going to put up with you not helping out around the house. You will be productive or you will get out. My wife has enough on her with four young ones to feed and clothe. She doesn't need you to add to her work."

"Four hands are better than two, Albert. You'll be shocked at how much more gets done with both of us here!"

Clara stepped into the room from the stairs, and went over to take down her knitting. She'd finished the Christmas gifts for everyone, but they all still needed some new socks, and that was her next task. She badly wanted to do the best thing for her children.

"I think it's so quaint how you use all of your free time to make things for the children, Tara. That's really nice of you."

Clara didn't correct the other woman's pronunciation of her name, because she knew she'd done it deliberately. "I enjoy doing things for my family."

Albert smiled at her, his knife slicing through the wood quickly and efficiently. He'd made more train cars for Robert's train and some small woodland creatures for Gertie. He hadn't known what to do for Natalie, so she'd suggested he make her a small bed to put her dolls on. She no longer played with dolls, but she liked to have them sitting out nicely.

He'd made Clarence a tool box and would slowly fill it with tools of his own. Clarence was proving to be a huge help around the house.

"What are you making tonight?" Clara asked Albert as she eyed the piece of wood.

Albert smiled. "I want to do just a couple more animals for Gertie's collection. She loves animals so much. I think this one will be a bunny."

Clara smiled. "She'll love it."

Mary looked at them both. "So I guess it's okay to talk now that the children are in bed?"

Clara nodded. "The only reason it wasn't before is Clarence really does need to study in the evenings. He spends every day helping Albert work, and I don't want him falling behind in his studies."

Mary looked at Albert. "It's nice of you to teach a boy who isn't even yours how to do hard work like that. I'm sure he slows you down a lot."

Albert shook his head. "Clarence doesn't slow me down at all. He's a huge help to me. This is the first winter that I've felt like I had a good handle on all the work."

"It's really nice of you to say that. I guess I never realized what a very nice man you are, Albert."

Clara watched the byplay between the two, disgusted. What was Mary trying to do?

"I honestly enjoy it. Clarence really does help. We're having to feed the cattle on the open range. I can slowly drive the sleigh through the field, and Clarence stands on the back, pitching hay to the animals. Before, I'd have to jump down and do it myself, and then drive a little further and do it again."

Mary shrugged. "I suppose."

Clara was done. She'd heard enough for the night. "I'm really sleepy. I think I'll go on to bed." She stood up and went to the shelf to put her hand work down.

Albert stood as well, putting his knife and wood on the top shelf as he did every night so there was no danger of Robert trying to play with it. "I'll join you." He looked at Mary. "Good night. We have breakfast at 5:30."

He didn't wait for her reply, and instead followed Clara into the bedroom, closing the door behind him. As he undressed, he said, "I'm so sorry she's being so difficult. I hope she leaves soon. I just can't kick her out, though. She's too much like Sally."

Clara nodded. "I do understand. I'll do my best to be pleasant to her."

He sighed. "She's not the most pleasant person in the world."

"I've dealt with worse." She quickly undressed and reached for her nightgown. His hand stopped her.

"I don't think you'll need that tonight," he whispered against her ear.

She laughed softly. "You don't?"

"No, I really don't." He pulled her into his arms to demonstrate how she'd stay warm without it.

CLARA FIXED BREAKFAST by herself and had the table set before anyone came down the stairs. Mary wasn't up. Clara sighed. "It's time for breakfast. Natalie, would you run upstairs and wake Aunt Mary?"

Natalie nodded. "Why didn't she get up and help with breakfast, Mama? If she's going to live here, she needs to do chores."

"Just wake her, Natalie." Clara wasn't up to explaining how some people didn't care enough to help others, but she'd have a long discussion with her daughter about it soon.

Albert and Clarence came in from milking the cows and collecting eggs. They stomped the snow off their feet. Albert leaned down to kiss her good morning. "You have snow on your eyelashes," she told him.

He laughed. "I guess I do. It's cold out there!" He looked around the room. "Where's Mary?"

"I just sent Natalie to wake her."

Albert let out a loud sigh. "You're going to have to ask her to do specific chores." He shook his head. "I don't think she's going to do anything around the house otherwise."

Clara nodded. "I can see that. I don't even ask the girls to do their chores. They know to just get up and do them."

"I know. They're both good girls."

He and Clarence washed their hands for supper, and they all took their places. They didn't bother to wait for Mary who still hadn't come down. As soon as Natalie was back they ate. Mary still wasn't down when Albert and Clarence left for the day. "We'll be here at noon."

Clara nodded. They came home for lunch most days, but occasionally Albert asked her to pack a lunch pail for them. "Lunch will be ready."

The dishes were done and the girls had finished two subjects of schoolwork, while Albert practiced writing his letters before Mary came down. She looked around. "When is breakfast?"

Clara looked up from rolling out a pie crust. "About two hours ago. We'll have lunch in another four hours or so." She said nothing else as she continued to roll out the crust.

Mary glared at her. "What about *my* breakfast?"

Clara shrugged. "You're welcome to make yourself something and do the dishes when you're done if you'd like. Otherwise, you need to wait until lunch time."

"I'll fix my own breakfast, but I won't do the dishes. That's what the girls are for." She pointed to the two girls who were sitting at the table silently watching the exchange.

"The girls do dishes three times per day. They've already done the breakfast dishes. If you cook for yourself, you'll need to clean it up."

"Why didn't you save me a plate?" Mary demanded.

"Albert told you breakfast was at five thirty. He told me not to do any extra work for you." Clara put the crust into a pie plate and carefully trimmed the edges. She then took a jar of apple pie filling she'd put up in September and opened it pouring it into the crust and quickly putting the top on, fluting the edges expertly.

She put the pie on top of the stove to be baked later. She had on a pot of beans for lunch, and she'd make corn bread to go with them. Supper. She had to figure something out for supper. She completely ignored her guest while she worked to get all the meals for the day in line for her family.

"Are you really not going to cook for me?" Mary asked.

Clara looked at her for a moment. "I'll cook for you when I cook for the rest of the family. If you want to eat food I've cooked, then be here for meals." She went down into the cellar to see what they had for supper. A pot pie sounded good, and she knew that Albert loved them. She grabbed the vegetables she'd need along with some of the salt pork.

She got to the main room in time to see Mary slamming her pots around. "What are you going to make?" she asked.

"I guess I'll make some eggs and bacon." She glared at Clara. "Where's the bacon?"

Clara smiled. "It's in the cellar. It stays colder down there and keeps longer." She pointed to the lantern she'd just used. "You're welcome to go get some."

Mary shook her head. "You can't ask me to go down there. Albert will be furious when I tell him."

"Albert won't mind a bit." Clara carefully peeled the potatoes and carrots she'd brought up.

Mary turned to the girls. "Which one of you girls wants to go fetch me some bacon?"

Natalie looked at the back of Clara's head for a moment. "I'll do it if my mama tells me to." Clara grinned at the words. Obviously Natalie realized Mary was playing games, and wasn't going to give in to her.

Gertie followed her older sister's lead, knowing she understood more about what was happening than she did. "I'm not going to do it unless Mama says."

Both girls continued to do their schoolwork. She didn't try to get Robert to go. Instead she stormed back up the stairs, leaving the pots strewn all over the kitchen. Clara sighed. She'd have to get that taken care of quickly before Albert came back.

She got everything chopped for their dinner and then put the beans she had soaking on to boil. She took the bacon she'd brought up earlier and cut it into pieces and dropped it in with the beans.

She was finished with the lunch preparations by the time Mary came back downstairs. "What are you making for lunch?"

Clara indicated the pot. "Beans with bacon and cornbread."

"When will it be done?"

"At noon." Clara moved to the sink and washed the few things she'd dirtied. She preferred not to leave everything for the girls to do after meals. Sitting down at the table, she asked, "How are your studies going this morning? Do either of you have any questions?"

Mary knew she'd been dismissed again and got even angrier. "I need you to fix me a bath and take it up to my room for me."

Clara looked at her. "The tub is leaning against the side of the house, and the stove is hot. You may use any pots you like."

Mary stood over her, looking down at her. "You really aren't going to ready a bath for me?"

"Albert told me that I'm not allowed to let you cause me extra work. I wasn't planning on carrying any water up the stairs today, so that definitely qualifies as extra work." Clara stood up and walked over to the window. "It's starting to snow harder. I hope Albert and Clarence make it back all right."

Mary stood there trying to figure out if the other woman was really not going to help her. "I need a bath."

Clara nodded. "You probably do after your travels. You're welcome to take one, or take a spit bath if you prefer. I'm not carrying water for you, though. You may be able to talk Albert into it this evening, but I doubt it." She shrugged to indicate she really didn't care whether the other woman got a bath or didn't.

"You know that you're the new person here, not me. Albert loved me when we were young, and I'm sure it won't take him long to realize he loves me now."

Clara shook her head. "Really? It doesn't matter who he loves. He's married to me." She turned and walked toward her bedroom, unwilling to let the children see how angry she was at the other women. She stopped before she reached the door. She couldn't leave Robert and the girls with Mary. The woman seemed unstable.

Instead, she got her mending basket down and started darning the stockings in it. Mary sat down across from her. She'd obviously given up on the ideas of bathing and eating. "What are you doing?"

Clara raised an eyebrow. "I'm mending socks." Had the woman never seen anyone work before?

"Why not just buy new ones? Is Albert poor?"

Clara blinked. "Out here it's not that simple. We make the most of everything we have. I would have thought it was the same in Texas."

Mary shrugged. "It was for most. I was a merchant's daughter. If I had a hole in my stocking, I got a new one."

"Well, I mend ours. I like to get the most for my money. Just because I have money today, doesn't mean I'll have it tomorrow. Anything could go wrong, so the smart thing to do is to always be frugal."

"You really believe that?"

Clara nodded. "I do. You're welcome to help me if you'd like. I have plenty of stockings that need to be mended."

Mary shook her head. "I don't do that type of work."

Clara studied the other woman carefully. "What type of work do you do?"

"I can cook when I feel like it. I had servants to do everything else."

"Servants? Really? Why don't you have servants now?"

Mary flushed. "My husband wasn't good with money. There was nothing left when he died."

"Which is why I'm frugal with my money." She continued darning the sock. "You should find something to do. Being idle will make you crazy."

Albert and Clarence stomped into the house. Clara looked at them. "Is everything okay? That storm is getting bad."

Albert shook his head. "It is bad. We got the cattle enough hay that they'll survive if the blizzard doesn't last too long. It's going to be a bad one, though." He stomped off his boots and hung his coat and hat while Clarence did the same.

Mary went to Albert. "Clara is being extremely unkind to me."

Albert's eyes met Clara's. "How is she being unkind?"

"She won't let me eat."

Clara bit her lip to keep from yelling at the other woman about her untruth. She knew both girls had listened to every word, though, so she wasn't going to argue. "Is that so?" Albert asked.

"It is. I told her I was hungry too."

Albert shrugged. "I'm sure you're welcome to make yourself something to eat or to wait for lunch. I know my wife won't withhold food from you for long."

"She won't even get me what I need to cook for myself or ask either girl to do it, and they won't help me unless she tells them to."

Albert looked at the girls, who were both watching with wide eyes to see if they'd be punished. He smiled at them. "Good girls." His eyes met Mary's. "If you're that hungry, I suggest you get your own food and cook it. Or just have some of the bread Clara made yesterday with butter on it. That wouldn't kill you." He thought of all the jam sandwiches he'd eaten with his children after Sally died. He thanked God for the hundredth time he had never married the worthless woman.

Mary sighed. "So you support her not fixing a meal for me? Or even getting me the ingredients I need?"

"I support my wife. No other words need to be spoken."

"I want you to take me to town."

Albert laughed. "I can't even work on the range in this storm. There's no way I'm driving to town and risking both of our necks."

"I want to go *now*." Mary's voice was just short of a yell.

Albert sighed. "Be my guest. Town is about eleven miles from here. You can walk that in a day or two. You'll be dead before you get there with this weather, but you're welcome to go."

He walked to where Clara was sitting at the table with her sewing. He pulled out the chair and sat across from her. "I'm done working at least for today and probably for tomorrow as well. Anything broken around the house that I need to take a look at?"

Clara smiled at him. Since the last storm, she'd been working on a list of things for him to do when the next blizzard hit. She hadn't thought of it the first time, and he'd made her crazy with his constant pacing and wanting to go out and work. He couldn't stand his hands being idle and made himself crazy when he couldn't work.

She jumped up and went into their bedroom to get the list for him. He took one glance at it and burst out laughing. "You really need all this done? Or are you just trying to find busy work for me?"

"All of it needs to be done." She smiled sweetly. "Today if possible."

He shook his head. Some of the things on the list were silly and some were useful. She'd actually put, "Read a book to Robert" on the list. Yes, it was something he rarely did, and something he should do more often, but something he needed to do that day? "I'll get to it. How long until lunch?"

"It'll be ready around noon. You have some time."

He stood up and walked toward the stairs. "I'll start on moving the dressers in the kids' rooms so you can sweep behind them. Will you be ready to sweep when I get everything moved?"

"I can be ready whenever you are!" she called. He stopped and turned around, going to get the broom to carry up the stairs with him. She watched him go, smiling happily. She was going to keep him busy during this storm if it killed her.

Clara turned to Clarence. "Get started on your schoolwork. You should be able to do a weeks' worth every day you're off. Then you can have some free time in the evenings.

Clarence nodded, going to the shelf to get his books. "Yes, ma'am."

Robert had followed Albert up the stairs. Clara noticed that anytime Mary was around he wanted to be close enough to touch either her or Albert. She'd always considered children the best judges of character. What did Robert know that she didn't?

Mary sat at the table with her and watched her work. "I'm bored. There's nothing to do here."

Clara nodded. "When the children tell me they're bored, I find them some chores to do. Would you like some chores, Mary?"

Mary sighed. "No, I don't want any chores." She watched everything Clara did. "Why did you give Albert a list of things to do? You shouldn't be ordering him around."

"Because he gets restless during storms. Staying busy is good for him."

Natalie stood then, stretching. "I finished my schoolwork, Mama. Is there anything I can do to help you?" Natalie wasn't usually the kind to offer to help, but she always did the chores she was given. Clara had a feeling that Natalie was tired of the way Mary was treating her and trying to show her how to be helpful and do chores.

"I'd love it if you went upstairs and swept after the furniture is moved." She smiled at her daughter. "Thank you, Natalie."

"I'm happy to help you, Mama. You do a lot for me." Natalie kissed Clara's cheek on her way to the stairs.

Clara watched her go with a smile. Moving had been very good for Natalie. She was a lot more focused on the things she needed to do now that she spent all her time at home with her family.

Mary snorted. "Did you talk to them all at breakfast and tell them to be perfect around me?"

Clara shook her head. "I didn't." She never once looked up and kept to the task at hand.

When Gertie finished her schoolwork, she jumped up. "I'm going to go help too." She ran up the stairs to join Albert, Robert, and Natalie.

Clara stood to mix the cornbread and get lunch finished. She shivered a bit as she looked at the snow blowing outside the window.

She was glad the house was as sturdy as it was, and she could feel no drafts. She looked over her shoulder at Mary who was still sitting at the table doing nothing. "Do you want to mix up the cornbread? You said you don't mind cooking."

Mary glared at her. "With the way I've been treated today? You really think that I'm going to help you cook?"

Clara shrugged and put the ingredients into the bowl, mixing them against her stomach. She'd get it done in no time. She and the girls did a good job in the house, and she didn't care if Mary helped or not.

Clara slid the cornbread into the oven and stirred the beans. She'd made more than usual because with Mary there, and having not eaten breakfast, she was sure they'd run out.

By the time lunch was ready, she'd set the table and the rest of the family was back downstairs. "Just about ready," she told Albert when he came down, Robert still clinging to his leg.

While they ate, Albert laughed about how dusty it was under the furniture. "You really did need that job done. I thought you were just having me do busy work, so I wouldn't be in your way."

Clara laughed softly. "There was a little of that mixed in, but those are jobs that are difficult for me to do, so while you're not working, I'd appreciate the help."

Mary wouldn't look at anyone throughout the meal; she just methodically shoveled food into her mouth. Finally, when she was finished, she leaned back in her chair. "I need you to take me to town as soon as the weather is clear enough."

Albert shrugged. "I'll do it if I can. The first day or two after a blizzard are busy with seeing to the cattle and making sure they're all right."

"So your cattle are more important than I am?" Mary asked indignantly.

Albert laughed. "My cattle are my livelihood. From what my girls tell me, you won't even raise a finger to bathe yourself. Why would I worry about you?"

Clara hid her grin. She loved that Albert was defending her. She loved it even more that the girls had made sure he knew how the other woman was treating her. Clara was nothing but kind, but she wouldn't go out of her way to do what the other woman wanted her to do.

After lunch, the girls jumped up to wash the dishes immediately. They'd always been good about doing their chores, but that day they were exceptional. She knew it was because of how Mary was treating her, and she couldn't help but smile at them as they worked.

Clarence settled in at the table to do some more schoolwork, while Albert went to the barn to get some tools he needed to complete one of the jobs she'd asked of him. "Skip that one if it means going outside in this," Clara suggested.

"I'll be fine. This isn't my first blizzard." Albert leaned down to press a quick kiss to her lips, making her realize that he really did care for her, if he'd kiss her so openly in front of the other woman.

Clara returned to her sewing, ignoring the other woman and her sullen look. She just didn't care to pay attention to her, when she was being so rude to her.

Mary watched everything she did that day, as if she were trying to find something to complain about, but there was nothing. Clara worked from the time she got up in the morning until she went to bed, and she wasn't going to worry about what the other woman thought about her.

The snow had stopped the following morning, and Albert was thrilled. "That was a short one. We may not have lost any cattle at all." He practically skipped out of the house with Clarence behind him.

Mary again wasn't up in time for breakfast, and Clara didn't put a portion aside for her. She wasn't going to do anything like that for someone who wasn't helping out at all.

That evening during dinner, Albert told Mary he'd take her to town the following morning. "Where are you planning to go?" he asked politely.

Mary shrugged. "I have nowhere to go, but I can't stay here with people who mistreat me."

"How have you been mistreated exactly?" he asked.

Mary glared at him. "I've already told you. No one will get a bath ready for me. No one will fix me a meal."

"You're eating a meal now," Albert pointed out logically.

"Yes, I am, but no one saved any breakfast for me."

"And no one will here. If you want to go to town, you need to be ready right after breakfast in the morning. I have some friends I'll introduce you to if you'd like." He didn't add that he was hoping they could make each other miserable.

She nodded regally. "Maybe one of them can use a wife or a lady's companion."

He laughed. "No one here needs a lady's companion. Men want wives though, and there just aren't enough women." He shrugged. "I'm sure even you can find a husband. Just make sure they don't see your personality until after they've said 'I do.'"

"I can't believe you just said that to me!"

"I can't believe no one's said it before." Albert stood up and walked to the door, shrugging into his coat. "I'm going to go make sure the horses will be warm enough through the night."

Mary watched him go with venom in her eyes. She looked at Clara. "I notice he didn't invite you to go with us."

Clara shrugged. "He'll probably take Clarence as well."

The girls worked on the dishes while Clara got her sewing. She wasn't going to listen to anything else the venomous woman had to say to her.

Chapter 7

THE FOLLOWING MORNING was tense. Clara had one of the girls wake Mary well before breakfast to be sure she was ready to go on time. Clara didn't want to spend another minute with the other woman under her roof.

As soon as breakfast was over, Albert sent Mary up the stairs to get her things. "We need to leave in fifteen minutes. Be ready."

Clara watched her go, happy that she was finally going to be out of her house. It seemed as if she'd been there for years, even though it had only been a few days. Clara couldn't help but wonder how much like her sister Sally had been. She'd probably ask him once Mary was gone, but she hadn't been willing to broach the subject with her there.

Clarence helped hitch up the team and ran back into the house to be sure Clara knew he was going with Albert. Clara fixed a lunch for them and smiled as she waved them off. The back of another woman's head had never looked quite so good to Clara.

ALBERT MADE SURE CLARENCE sat in the front seat of the sleigh between him and Mary. "He should sit in the back. He's making it crowded up here, and he just a child," Mary protested.

Albert shrugged. "I don't want him to get cold in the back. He's sharing our body heat this way."

"What do you care? He's not even your son. He's just the son of that terrible woman you married." She shook her head. "I can't believe you married her anyway. I'm sure you'd have waited for me if you'd known I was coming, but couldn't you have found someone better? It's almost insulting!"

Albert looked at her with surprise. "You think I would have waited for you instead of marrying Clara? What have I done to make you think that?"

Mary laughed. "Don't deny it, Albert! You loved me."

"That's true. Loved. Past tense. I stopped loving you the day you told me you couldn't wait for me. It didn't take me long to realize that Sally was the one I'd loved all along. Sally was everything you weren't. She was a hard worker, sweet and loving. You...you're poison to everyone you see or touch. I'm so glad to get you out of my house." Albert drove staring at the road ahead of him, wondering what Clarence thought of the conversation he was having with Mary. "My new wife is a better wife than you could ever dream of being. She puts the children and me before herself in everything. I've never met such an unselfish woman in my life."

Mary looked at him and gasped as if offended. "Are you calling me selfish, Albert Hanson?"

"Well, I didn't say it in so many words, but you are one of the most selfish people I've ever met. You think of no one but yourself. You came here without giving me notice to try and take over my life. I didn't want you here, Mary. Even if Clara hadn't been here, I'd have wanted to toss you out on your ear."

Mary sputtered for a moment, staring at him over Clarence's head. "Clara doesn't hold a candle to me or my sister."

Albert laughed aloud. "Have you ever heard the expression, 'Pretty is as pretty does?' Clara was attractive to me when she arrived, because she has a pretty face. Now? She's the most beautiful woman I've ever met, because she has a good attitude about everything she does. She told me not to buy her anything for Christmas, but she stays up late every night making special gifts for the children. I don't know what she's done for me, but I'm sure she's done something that will be wonderful, because it's who she is." He shook his head. "I almost feel sorry for you. You expect every man in the world to fall at your feet because you have a pretty face. It's not going to happen, because you don't have the personality and work ethic to back up that pretty face."

"How dare you!"

"It all needed to be said. Do you have money for a train ticket to Texas?" Albert asked.

"Of course, I don't. If I had money, I wouldn't have shown up on your doorstep, now would I?"

"I'll buy your ticket."

"To where?" Mary asked shrilly. "I have nowhere to go! No one wants me. Mama and Papa are dead!"

Albert shrugged. "Where am I taking you then? If not to the train station?"

"I don't know. I just had to get away from that...woman you married."

He sighed. "Maybe there will be someone in town who will hire you to do...something."

"Are you now implying that I'm not good for anything?"

He shrugged. "I'll let you make that decision." He stopped because they'd reached the mercantile. "Maybe someone will be advertising for something you can do."

He jumped down and waited for Clarence, but left her to get down on her own. He didn't like how she'd talked about his wife. The woman was a real pain in his behind, and he wasn't going to mess with her any longer. He walked into the mercantile and called to Samuel. "Anyone looking for a woman to do some work for them?"

Samuel shook his head slowly. "No one that I know of. I know a few of the men around town are thinking about sending off for mail order brides, though. You got someone you're trying to get rid of?"

Albert grinned. "My first wife's sister needs somewhere to go. She's unhappy at my house, and she has nowhere else. Any suggestions?"

Samuel took a piece of paper and calmly made a list which he then handed to Albert. "There's a list of men that I know are looking for brides. Go talk to them. Maybe one of them will take her off your hands."

Albert let out a low laugh. "That's what I'm looking for." He glanced down at the list. "No one closer to town? I want to dump her and go back home." He sighed. "It's going to be a long day."

Clarence looked at him. "Pa, why does Aunt Mary hate Mama so much?"

Albert shook his head. "There are just some people in this world who have no love inside them. I think Mary is one of those." He strode toward the wagon with Clarence trailing behind him. Mary was still sitting on the seat of the sleigh.

"I see you finally remembered me."

Albert shrugged. "We're ready to go on. There are no jobs for women in town, but there are several men around looking for a wife. We'll go visit them and see which one will take you."

"Take me? You make me sound like a terrible burden you can't wait to be rid of. Albert, how can you treat me this way?"

He ignored her question as he tipped his hat at a friend as they drove south out of town. There had to be someone who wanted sex so badly, he'd marry a shrew like Mary, didn't there?

It was an hour before they arrived at the first man's house. Albert jumped down, telling Clarence to stay put. He wandered around for a moment hoping he could find the man, and he wouldn't be out on the range. Finally he spotted his friend, Eli King, coming out of the barn. He raised his hand in greeting.

Eli walked toward him eyeing the sleigh. He held his hand out for the other man to shake. "Good to see you, Albert. You doing all right?"

"I have a slight dilemma. I sent off for a mail order bride a few months back, and she's here and the best wife I could have asked for. A few days ago, my late wife's sister showed up, widowed, thinking she could keep house for me. She spent her last dime on train travel." Albert shrugged. "I don't really know what to do with my former sister-in-law, but she'd like to marry again. You in the market for a wife or a housekeeper?"

Eli looked at the sleigh and saw the pretty woman sitting in the front. "What's wrong with her?"

Albert laughed loudly. "What makes you think there's something wrong with her?"

"I know you, and I know you'd keep her if there was any way it was possible. Why can't she stay at your house?"

Albert sighed. "Because she's mean and lazy and is doing her best to make my wife's life difficult."

Eli shook his head. "Thanks but no thanks. I'm sure someone will take her, but I don't need no crazy woman in my life."

"She's not crazy!"

"Sounds crazy to me. Thanks for thinking of me. If you get a good woman in, look me up."

Albert grinned. "I'm kind of glad you said 'no,' but I felt the need to ask you first. Some men are willing to put up with anything for regular sex."

"I'm not one of them. Bring me back a good one."

"I don't get women in every day." Albert walked back toward the sleigh with Eli beside him. He introduced his friend to Clarence and Mary. "This is my former sister-in-law, Mary, and my new son, Clarence. Clarence is more help around the ranch than I ever imagined an eight year old would be."

"Nice to meet you, ma'am, Clarence." Eli tipped his hat politely. He turned to Albert, and they clasped gloved hands together. "I'd love to meet your new wife. Invite me over for a good home-cooked meal sometime, will ya?"

Clarence smiled. "My mama's the best cook around."

Albert nodded. "She is. Why don't you come over for Christmas dinner? We'll eat around two so you can get home before dark. I'd love to introduce you."

Eli grinned. "I can't wait to meet the woman that put the sparkle back in your eye."

Albert climbed back into the sleigh, and the three of them drove off. He looked at his list and headed to the man who was closest. Hopefully he'd be more interested in Mary than Eli had been.

"Where exactly are we going, Albert?" Mary asked finally.

Albert looked at her. "I'm trying to find you a place to stay. Either a man who needs a wife or a housekeeper."

She looked over her shoulder. "Why not him?"

Albert shrugged. "He didn't want you."

Mary stared at him in shock. "What do you mean he didn't want me?"

"He said he doesn't have the patience to put up with a woman like you." Albert shrugged.

"He didn't see me before he said that, though."

Albert laughed. "He saw you just fine. He just doesn't want a woman who won't work and put him first. There's a man that will. We just have to find him."

It was almost suppertime when they finally found a man who would take her. Albert had begun to worry he'd never find anyone. He'd been through over half of his list at that point. He pulled up in front of Frank Rivers house and jumped down, thankful he wouldn't need to hunt this man down, because he should be home for supper.

Frank wasn't a particular friend of his, so he didn't mind if he decided to take Mary on, but he wouldn't lie to him either. He went to the door and knocked while the other two sat in the cold sleigh. If Frank didn't want her, he'd have to drive home and try again in a couple of days. He needed to get some work done before he could lose another full day.

Frank came to the door and looked at him oddly. "Hello, Albert. How can I help you?"

Albert smiled. This was one of the men who had been in the mercantile and had made rude comments about him taking a new wife. "My first wife's twin sister came to town. Her husband died, and she thought she could keep house for me. I didn't need a housekeeper, because I have a wife, so I'm looking to see if someone around here could use a wife or housekeeper."

Frank's eyes widened. "Your first wife was a beauty. I'll look at her for sure." He looked at Albert suspiciously. "You don't want to keep her for a bit? Have her help your wife with chores?"

Albert shook his head. "My house is too full as it is. I know you're looking for a wife, so I thought you might be interested."

"Can she cook?"

Albert shrugged. "She hasn't cooked for me in a good fifteen years. Why don't you ask her to come in and cook something for you? See how it goes?" He hoped he and Clarence could get a meal out of it as well. It was suppertime, and they'd had to share their lunch meant for two among three people.

"That's a good idea. Get her in here." Frank watched as Albert went to the sleigh and invited Clarence and Mary to come in. Frank's eyes widened as he saw the woman in question. When she was close, he smiled his biggest smile, showing off the wide gap between his front teeth. "Can you cook?"

Mary nodded emphatically. "I'm a wonderful cook."

Albert said nothing as the man invited the three of them inside. He took the seat that was indicated and sat beside Clarence at the table while Frank crossed his arms over his chest. "Cook then. Cook for all four of us, and if I like what I taste, then I'll consider marrying you."

Mary gasped with surprise. "You're making me audition to marry you?"

Frank shrugged. "Looks like you don't have much of a choice, now do you? Cook, and I'll see if I want you around."

Mary spun away from him, tears pricking her eyes. She rummaged for some food and came up with almost nothing. "How do you expect me to cook when you don't have any food?"

Frank waved to the trap door in the floor. "There's food down there. Fetch it and cook." He took a seat beside Albert and waited for the woman to do as he'd told her.

Mary huffed as she grabbed a lantern, opened the trap door, and went down into the cellar. She came back up the stairs with her arms full of potatoes, bacon, and a basket of eggs. Not one of the men moved to help her, and she glared at them.

She hurried to the stove, using a bit of lard to melt in the frying pan, while she peeled the potatoes and cut them up.

She fried the bacon and potatoes and then added eggs. Within minutes she had a good meal cooked, and the four of them gobbled it down. When he had wiped his mouth with his sleeve, Frank said, "Yeah, she'll do. I'll keep her, Albert."

Mary glared at him. "Don't you think you should ask me first?"

Frank shrugged. "I don't guess so. Albert doesn't want you, and from what I can tell, no one else does either."

Mary looked at Albert. "Are you going to make me stay here and marry this man?"

"I don't know what you want me to do, Mary. There are no jobs available in town. You don't want me to put you on a train somewhere. You won't help my wife around the house. You either stay here and marry him, or figure something else out. I'm done." Albert looked at Frank. "You mind if Clarence and I spend the night here? I don't think we can make it home safely this late at night with the snow."

Frank nodded. "That's fine. I've got a couple of spare rooms. No sheets on the beds, but Mary can take care of that after the dishes are done."

"You expect me to do the dishes? I just cooked dinner!"

Frank laughed. "I expect you to cook and do dishes three times a day and keep the house clean. If kids come along they'll be your responsibility too. Get on it, woman."

Mary reluctantly walked to the basin and washed the dishes, grumbling all the while. When she was finished, she made both of the beds. "Where do I sleep tonight?" she asked, her voice sharp with anger.

"In one of the spare rooms. I'll have you all to myself tomorrow night." He leered at her, and she ran from the room, choosing one of the rooms and slamming the door hard.

Albert looked at Frank. "You're not going to mistreat her, are you?"

Frank shook his head. "Course not. She just needs to know I'm boss from the beginning. Kinda like when you're training a horse."

Albert chuckled. "You two are going to have an interesting life together."

CLARA DIDN'T EXPECT them back for lunch, but when it was almost supper time and the two were still out, she became worried. She served supper, but kept glancing out the window every few minutes to see if they were home. She put two huge portions of dinner in the oven, and watched as the girls did the dishes. When it was time to put the children to bed, she was almost shaking with fear, but did her best to not let the girls know it.

"Mama, where are they? Do you think something happened?" Natalie asked.

"I'm sure everything is fine. They probably realized it was too dark to come home, so they stayed in town."

Natalie eyed her skeptically but didn't argue. She got into bed without another word and waited while Clara kissed first Gertie and then her. "Good night, Mama."

Clara turned at the door and smiled at both the girls. "Good night. Sleep sweet."

She closed the door behind her, hurrying down the stairs to continue her vigil. What would she do if something happened to them? She couldn't run a ranch by herself. She sat in her chair at the table and knitted, knowing she had to do something to take her mind off things. Finally, when it was well past midnight, she went to her bed.

She lay awake in the darkness with tears streaming down her face. She couldn't imagine what life would be like without either of them. Albert...how had she come to love the man? She'd promised herself she wouldn't love anyone the way she'd loved Nathan, and yet here she was. Lying in the dark crying over him.

She slept for less than an hour and woke early, her stomach more than a little upset. She wasn't sure if it was from lack of sleep, or from worrying about her men, but she knew something was making her sick. She fixed breakfast, automatically making the same amount she made for all six of them and laughing at herself. She forced herself to eat a small amount of dry toast, but she vomited it almost immediately. Both of the girls knew how worried she was and watched her carefully.

ALBERT WOKE LATER THAN usual the next morning in the room he was sharing with Clarence. He could hear pans being banged around in the kitchen and assumed Frank had told Mary to get out of bed and feed them all. He smiled. He'd solved his and Clara's problem, but it looked like Frank was going to be able to handle Mary after all.

He went down to breakfast and ate the pancakes Mary had made. She hadn't exaggerated. She was a good cook. She wasn't Clara, but she was almost as good. He put his hat on after breakfast. "Clarence, it's time for us to get home. Your ma must be worried sick."

Mary hurried to the door. "You can't leave me here. Can't you at least go to the wedding? I don't think I should stay here with a stranger that I'm not even married to."

Albert let out a loud sigh before nodding reluctantly. He could see the problem with being alone with a man she barely knew. "We'll follow the two of you into town."

She shook her head. "No, I want to ride with you."

"We either follow you and Frank into town and stay for the wedding, or we go on home now. Either way would be just fine with me." He hoped she'd be angry with him and just tell him to go.

Mary looked like she was about to cry. "Follow us into town, then. My sister would not be happy with you, though."

Albert laughed. "Your sister knew you for who you were. She wouldn't care one lick."

He waited until the couple was ready, and he and Clarence followed them into town. They witnessed the wedding, and Albert couldn't help but laugh when Mary stomped on Frank's foot after the ceremony. As soon as they were pronounced man and wife, Albert shook hands with Frank. "I hope you two are happy together."

Frank shrugged. "We will be."

Albert led Clarence to the sleigh, and they turned toward home finally. He looked at his pocket watch. It was going to be afternoon before they got back. Poor Clara would be worried sick.

AS THE DAY PROGRESSED, Clara did her best to keep to her normal schedule. She baked bread as soon as the dishes were done and did the laundry, including all the linens, hanging it in the basement. She even stripped the curtains off the windows and washed them so she wouldn't have to think about anything. The physical labor kept her mind off her worries.

As she was cleaning off the table after lunch, she heard the horses and rushed to the window. She sighed with relief. There they were. She threw the door open and rushed outside into the cold. She wore no shoes or coat, but she didn't care. She needed to know her family was fine.

"Everything all right?" she called.

Albert nodded. "I need to see to the horses, but then I'll be right in."

Clara went back into the house and pulled the remains of lunch from the oven, setting the table for the two of them. She was so relieved they were all right she had tears rolling down her face. She'd never take anyone for granted again.

When they came back into the house, Clara didn't wait for Albert to remove his coat, and instead threw herself at him, hugging him tightly. "I was so worried."

Albert wrapped his arms around her, holding her close. "I'm sorry. Mary was...difficult. She didn't want to go anywhere and demanded I find her a place to live in town. I didn't feel right about sending her back to Texas with no family there, so I took her to some of the ranches around town, trying to find her a job as a housekeeper, or find someone stupid enough to take her as a bride."

Clara nodded. "I should have guessed it was something like that."

Albert rubbed the back of his neck, shrugging out of his coat. He walked to the basin and washed his hands, before taking a seat at the table. He continued his story, while she served lunch to both him and Clarence. "It was late before I finally found someone who would take her as a bride, and I didn't think it would be safe to travel home. So I stayed the night with Frank, my friend who married her this morning, and thought to come home first thing this morning. Of course, then she decided that she couldn't be alone with the man until they were legally married, so we followed them back into town and stayed for the wedding." He shook his head. "I should have just dumped her in town, but she looks so much like Sally, I just couldn't bring myself to do it."

Clara sat down across from him and took his hand. "I'm just glad you're okay."

"You're not angry that we worried you?" His eyes searched hers carefully for any sign of anger.

She shrugged. "You're not dead, so I'm elated. I might get mad later."

He laughed softly. "You look like you barely slept."

"I only got about an hour. I couldn't stop worrying about you." She looked around. "I got a lot of cleaning done while I worried, though."

He squeezed the hand she held. "House looks great." His eyes searched hers. "Thank you for caring enough to worry about me."

She sighed. "How could I do anything else?"

While he ate, he told her about Frank and how he'd demanded that Mary fix him a good meal before he'd agree to marry her.

Clara bit her lip to keep from laughing, but after a moment, she couldn't keep it in any longer. She burst out laughing, holding her side. It didn't take long for Albert to join her. She had tears rolling down her face. "It sounds like he's the perfect husband for her."

Albert wiped a tear from his own eye grinning at her. "He is the perfect husband for her. He's going to keep her hopping." He finished his meal and pulled Clara into a tight hug. "Thank you for not being angry when I took her to town without you. You were really good about her being here, even though I know she had to be making you absolutely crazy."

Clara smiled, hugging him close. "I'm glad she's gone. I'll say that now."

He grinned. "We're all glad she's gone."

Chapter 8

CLARA'S PREPARATIONS for Christmas were in full swing. Albert had told her about inviting one of his friends for Christmas dinner, and he'd brought her a turkey, which she'd prepared to cook on Christmas morning.

She found that she had a little less energy every day, and her stomach always seemed to be rioting against her. She was in her bedroom wrapping the gifts when she realized what must be wrong. She hadn't had her flow since October, and it was now Christmas. Why hadn't she seen it sooner? She was carrying his baby. She didn't even know if Albert wanted another child. They already had enough mouths to feed.

She worried, but decided she wasn't going to put off telling him. She'd heard tell of a lot of women who would wait for a special occasion to announce their pregnancy, but she'd tell him that night. The next day was Christmas Eve, and he'd work then. On Christmas, they'd go to church in the morning, and have their Christmas dinner shortly after church. She wanted telling him out of the way, before their festivities.

After the children were in bed that evening, she put her hand on her stomach, thinking about what it would be like to have a baby around the house. She knew both girls would enjoy having a younger sibling. Natalie had really come around and loved being there. Clarence had loved Montana from the minute he'd gotten off the train.

She walked down the stairs quickly, holding her hand to her belly as she did. She saw him sitting quietly at the table, carving something small. "Is that another Christmas gift?" she asked.

"No. I'm just messing around." He set the wood down and smiled at her. "You happy?"

She nodded. "I'm really excited to see the children's faces on Christmas morning. They'll be thrilled."

"They will." His hand reached up to stroke her cheek. "I'm so glad you and the children came out here. You were just what we needed in our lives."

"How would you feel about more children? If they happened to come along?" she asked.

He looked at her surprised. "I hadn't really thought about it. You didn't have children for so long that I figured you were past that."

She shrugged. "I thought so too." She looked down at her hands. "I guess not."

"You mean...?" His eyes were wide as he stared at her.

"Yes, we're expecting. Probably about July." She bit her lip, worried that he would be unhappy with her condition.

His face lit up in a grin. "I think that's exactly what we need. We have your kids and my kids, but we need one that's ours, too." He pulled her into his arms and kissed her softly. "I love the idea."

"I wasn't sure how you'd feel. I didn't think I could have more children, just because I hadn't, and I had symptoms for a while, but never really connected it." She rested her hand against his cheek, thrilled that he wasn't angry with her. "I'm glad you're happy about the baby."

"There's no reason to ever be sad about a baby. If all of ours were under five, and you had another coming, that would be hard, but it would still be a blessing. I love children."

She nodded. "I do too."

"So when should we tell the children?" he asked.

"Why don't we tell them at breakfast in the morning? I'd love to start making tiny little blankets and clothes tomorrow. They'll be hard to explain if the children don't know about the baby."

He chuckled. "That would be hard to explain." He shook his head. "I'm having a hard time wrapping my mind around this. We're really having a baby!"

Clara couldn't believe the joy in his face as they talked about the child. "Do you know where the closest midwife is?"

"The one Sally used is just a couple of miles up the road. You'll be fine."

She sighed and nodded. "I admit, my biggest fear about moving here was how far we'd be from the nearest town. I wasn't sure I'd feel safe without having a doctor I could run to."

"Well, if it comes to it, I'm sure I could help. I've helped the horses and cows give birth on several occasions."

She made a face. "I'm sure you're qualified, but not so sure how I'd feel about it. I'd rather you didn't see me that way."

He grinned. "Sally said the same thing. It's not like I've never seen you before."

She blushed. "Maybe you have seen me, but you haven't seen a baby coming out of me, and you're just not going to!" She leaned back in her chair and folded her arms across her chest.

He laughed softly. "Whatever you want. I'm just glad we're having a baby!"

"I was worried you wouldn't want it. That you'd think we had enough mouths to feed."

"Not at all. I mean, I don't want to feed more mouths, but I'm thrilled we're having another child. We make enough. We'll be fine."

She rested her hand on his knee. "I'm glad."

"Have you been sick a lot?"

She nodded. "Mainly in the mornings, but it happens in the middle of the afternoon too. It started the morning that you weren't here because you were driving Mary. I thought it was just nerves because I was worried about you." She shrugged with a smile. "I guess not."

He stood and took her hand, leading her to the bedroom. "I'm happy for the baby. I hope the pregnancy is easy for you."

"The others were. Of course, I was much younger then."

"It's not like you're ancient now. Why, we could easily have another four or five children." He quickly undressed and readied himself for bed, climbing in and watching her undress. His eyes watched her carefully, as if he was trying to see every little change in her body. "You don't look pregnant."

She laughed as she pulled a nightgown over her head. "You say that as if it's a bad thing. I would think that would thrill you."

He shrugged. "It never bothered me when Sally became huge with child, and I'm sure it won't bother me when you do either. It's my child changing your body."

She climbed into bed beside him and snuggled into his arms. She knew she should probably be disappointed that he didn't love her, but she was just thrilled that he wasn't unhappy about the baby. "I can't wait to tell the children. Natalie and Gertie are going to be really excited."

His hands stroked her. "I guess it's a good thing the girls moved into a bedroom together. Now there will be room for the baby."

Clara sighed happily. "There will be. And we won't have to do it later."

He cupped her cheek and turned her face up to his. "Thank you for giving me a child."

She rubbed her cheek against his chest, content.

He stroked her back and reached over to turn down the lantern and plunged them into darkness. Kissing the top of her head, he whispered, "Good night."

She was already sleeping.

CLARA MADE BREAKFAST the following morning, very excited that they would be telling the children about the baby at breakfast. Once they were all seated, and Albert had said the prayer, she said, "Papa and I have something to tell all of you."

The children looked at each other. "Please tell me Aunt Mary isn't coming back!" Natalie blurted out.

Clara laughed. "No, Aunt Mary is not coming back." She smiled at her daughter, and then her eyes moved between the children. "You tell them, Albert."

"We're having another baby," he said, his face spread into a wide grin.

Natalie looked between the two of them. "Are you serious? That's your news?"

Clara nodded. "Not what you expected?" she asked.

Natalie shook her head adamantly, an angry look on her face.

Gertie jumped up and ran to hug Clara. "I want a sister!"

Albert smiled. "We can't control whether the baby is a boy or a girl. We'll feel blessed with either."

Clarence didn't comment, but he didn't look upset by the news either. Robert smiled. "I won't be the youngest anymore?"

"You won't be the youngest. Does that make you happy?" Clara asked.

Robert frowned. "I don't know. Do I have to share my train?"

"Yes, you do," Clara told him. "You'll have to share all of your toys whether it's a girl or a boy."

Robert gave a long suffering sigh. "I suppose I can put up with that so I won't have to be the youngest anymore."

"Can I help you change diapers, Mama?" Gertie asked.

"That's a duty I'm happy to share!" Clara kept her gaze on her older daughter, wondering what was going through her mind. She'd have to be sure to get her aside and talk to her sometime that day.

Albert pushed back form the table. "Thank you for the fine breakfast, Clara."

Clara nodded at him, glad he'd started to come around and compliment each of the meals she fixed. "I'm glad you enjoyed it."

Albert and Clarence put on their winter coats and left. Clara looked at Robert. "I want you to play quietly for a moment. Gertie, would you clear the table and get started on washing the dishes while Natalie and I make the beds? I know it's not how we usually do things, but just for today, would you mind?"

Gertie shook her head, eager to please as always.

Clara climbed the stairs behind Natalie, wondering what was going on. She was worried about the cold reception their news had gotten from Natalie, because she was usually so excited about children. When they reached the girls room, they each went to opposite sides of the bed to make it. "What's wrong, Natalie? Aren't you happy about the baby?"

Natalie shrugged. "I like babies."

"What's wrong then? I don't understand why you're not happier." Clara plumped the pillow and rested it back onto the bed.

"I feel like you like Gertie and Robert more than me already. If you have another baby, you'll never have time for me!" Natalie blurted the words out, looking very upset.

Clara sighed. "How could I like anyone better than my firstborn daughter?" She sat on the bed and patted the spot next to her. "The others are younger and need my attention more. I have to give them more of my time. With this baby coming, I'm going to need your time. Expecting a baby makes a woman a lot more tired than usual. Cooking breakfast in the mornings is making me sick to my stomach. I may need you to do some of those things for me." She gave Natalie a quick hug. "I'm so proud of the young woman you've become."

Tears sprang into Natalie's eyes. "I'll help as much as I can, Mama. And...I want to help change diapers too."

Clara laughed. "I promise there will be enough diapers for all of us to take our turns."

NATALIE WAS UP EARLIER than usual the following morning, which was Christmas. She helped Clara get the turkey ready for the oven, and then she suggested Clara sit down while she cooked.

Clara smiled at her daughter. "I'm going to go wake everyone and help the two little ones get ready for church. Thank you for being such a good daughter to me."

Albert was already outside milking the cows and collecting eggs. He was startled to see Natalie at the stove instead of Clara. "Is your mama sick?"

Natalie shook her head as she carefully turned the bacon. "She told me yesterday that cooking breakfast is making her sick to her stomach, so I did it for her." She shrugged as if cooking breakfast for the family was something she did every day.

Albert smiled, giving her a one-armed hug. Natalie had always been stand-offish toward him, and he didn't feel like he was getting a chance to get to know her at all. "Your mama and I appreciate all the hard work you do around here. You're a good daughter."

Natalie looked at him with surprise. "Thank you, Papa."

He turned away and grinned as he went into the bedroom to put on his church clothes. It was the first time Natalie had called him Papa, and it felt good to him. He put on his clothes and joined the family at the table. Both boys were in their suits, and Gertie was in one of the pretty dresses Clara had made for her.

Last Christmas had been terrible, with his wife being so ill, and the children so sad. He was glad God had blessed them so much in the past year, and he smiled at Clara. She was a beautiful woman and a good wife. He didn't know when he'd come to love her, but he hadn't been able to stop himself. She was the wife he needed. The children loved her, and the fact that she was carrying his child was just icing on the cake.

After breakfast, they opened their gifts one by one. They had Robert go first, because he was the youngest, and he was thrilled with his new hat and gloves. He tried the gloves on and clapped his hands together with excitement. He squealed with excitement when he saw the train. "Oh, thank you, Papa!"

His sisters had worked together to make him a new quilt for his bed. He immediately covered up with it, his eyes wide with surprise. "Thank you!"

Gertie went next, exclaiming over her new sweater and the figurines her papa had made her. Natalie and Clarence had worked together, and Clarence had built a small doll bed, while Natalie had made a doll sized quilt for it. Gertie hugged everyone, thanking them over and over for the wonderful gifts.

Clarence was thrilled with the new coat, hat, and gloves his mother had made him. The toolbox Albert fashioned made his eyes light up with excitement. Albert had even purchased him a hammer and saw of his very own. The girls had made him a pair of socks. "I've never had a better Christmas," he exclaimed.

Natalie smiled happily when she opened the sweater that matched Gertie's. "Now we can look alike at church today!" She loved her new doll bed, and laughed that she'd been made the same thing as Gertie had. Gertie had made her a pillow for their bed, because she always said one wasn't enough. Clarence had given her a small book of poems he'd seen in the mercantile.

When it was Clara's turn to open her gifts, she smiled looking at them. "I really didn't expect anything!"

Albert shook his head. "After all the trouble you went to for everyone else, there was no way I was going to let you go without a gift yourself."

The girls had given her a doily for her dresser that they'd crocheted the lace for. She smiled as she looked at their imperfect stitches and knew she'd treasure it all the more for them. Clarence gave her his gift next. It was a small glass squirrel. She'd always loved to watch squirrels and when Clarence was little, she'd made up stories about squirrels for him.

When Albert handed her his gift, her heart skipped a beat. She carefully opened the brown wrapping paper and peeked inside. She put her hand to her chest and exclaimed happily when she saw what it was. "Oh, thank you!" It was just like the brooch she'd had to sell right before they'd left Beckham. She'd always regretted doing it, but she'd had no choice. "It's exactly like the one I sold."

"I'm glad," Albert told her. His eyes on hers let her know that he cared, more than just a little bit for her.

Clara pinned the brooch at the neck of her blouse, wishing she had a small mirror so she could see how it looked. She stood and walked around the table, kissing Albert's cheek. "It's lovely."

He smiled at her. "It looks as beautiful on you as I'd envisioned."

She flushed. She hadn't expected praise for her appearance from him. "Thank you."

She moved back around to sit in the spot she'd occupied previously, thrilled that he had given her the compliment. The children each gave him a gift. The girls had worked together to make him a scarf, taking turns knitting between chores. Clarence had sharpened his saw carefully for him one day when he was left at home. "I noticed it was rusty and gave it a good cleaning and sharpened it for you. I didn't know what else you needed."

Albert had smiled at him. "This was the perfect gift. I thought I was going to have to do it myself within the next week or so, and I wasn't looking forward to missing out on work. Thank you, son."

Clarence had beamed with pride. "You're welcome, Pa."

Clara took the package she'd wrapped and pushed it across the table to Albert. He carefully untied the string and looked down at what was inside. A smile transformed his face. He looked at the stocking cap and pulled the gloves onto his hands. "These will be wonderful this winter. Thank you."

Clara grinned and pushed the smaller package at him. "You're welcome."

"What's this? You already gave me a gift."

"I made you a couple of gifts, but I wanted to buy you something special as well." She shrugged like it didn't matter.

He opened the gift and turned the knife over in his hand. "I thought it would be good for your whittling. The one you have has a nick in the blade," she told him.

Albert shook his head. "This is beautiful. I don't need anything nearly this fancy." He smiled as his finger traced the cowboy on the handle.

"I thought it would make it more special when you made something if you carved it with that."

"I love it." He stared down at it resting in the palm of his hand. "I've never seen anything like it. Thank you." He'd never been given anything nearly so grand. His new wife thought of everything. He had loved his first wife, but she was right. He could love one and then love another after she was gone. He needed to tell her.

Clara jumped to her feet. "We need to go if we don't want to be late for church. Is everyone ready?"

Natalie was the only one not dressed in church clothes. She'd been afraid to get them dirty as she cooked breakfast. "It'll just take me a minute to change, Mama."

The next few minutes were frantic as they rushed out the door. Albert and Clarence went out to hitch up the sleigh, and Clara helped the two younger children into their coats, hats, and mittens.

The ride to church was enjoyable. They sang Christmas songs as they drove. It was Clara's first time at the church in town, and she met so many people, she felt as if her head would spin. She stiffened up when she saw Mary with her new husband. She tried to turn away, but Mary hurried to her.

"Please let me come back to live in your house. I'll help with every chore and never behave badly again."

Clara looked at the other woman, not sure of what to say. She didn't want to see anyone suffer, but she certainly didn't want to have to be saddled with the harridan ever again. Albert stepped up behind her and came to her rescue. "You're married now. You'll go home with your husband."

Frank stepped up behind Mary. "You complaining about me, wife?"

Mary quickly shook her head. "Of course not."

Frank shrugged. "She sure complains a lot to others about how terrible of a husband I am, but she doesn't complain in bed at night." He waggled his brows at Albert.

"I think it's time for us to go," Albert said, slipping his arm around Clara's waist and gathering the children. "I'm sure we'll see you around town."

When they arrived home, Clara and the girls rushed around to get Christmas dinner ready. Eli was the first real guest she'd serve in her new home, so Clara wanted everything to be perfect. When Eli arrived, she gave him the foot of the table while she sat at Albert's right. Albert said a prayer thanking God for his bounty, and they ate together.

Eli turned to Clara. "I've heard good things about you. How do you like Montana?"

Clara smiled. "I think it's a beautiful place. Do you think it will be a state soon?"

"Just a matter of time. Any other women like you back East who want to come out here and marry? I could use a mail order bride myself if she's as sweet and pretty as you are." He took a bite of food. "And as good a cook. I need a mail order bride who's a good cook."

Clara laughed. "I'm sure they could find someone for you. Before you go, I'll give you the address of the agency I used." She smiled at Albert who shook his head.

"You never know who you'll end up with when you use an agency to find a bride." Albert shrugged. "If you're willing to take the risk, we'll help you find someone."

Eli nodded. "I want that address."

The feast she'd prepared was devoured quickly, and they all sat around for a while after the dishes were done, talking. Clara worked on a tiny sweater while they men compared ranch stories.

Eli left before it was full dark. "I've been gone too long already," he told Albert. "Thank you for inviting me. I haven't spent Christmas with anyone but my dog in years."

Clara stood. "We're glad you came. Write a letter to Elizabeth," she said nodding to the paper in his hand. "I'd love to see you have a bride of your own next Christmas."

Eli smiled. "Thank you for a wonderful meal, Mrs. Hanson. I was the luckiest man around to be invited." He looked at Albert. "Well, second luckiest. Someone gets to see your pretty face and eat your cooking every day."

Clara blushed, looking down. "I'm glad you enjoyed it."

Clarence and Albert walked Eli out to his sleigh and did the evening chores before coming back inside. When they came back with the milk, Clara asked, "Is anyone hungry yet?"

Albert patted his stomach. "I couldn't eat anything yet. Maybe you could make something simple in a couple of hours. Like eggs? Or pancakes? I don't see any of us wanting another big meal."

"I'll do that then."

The children were all playing together, which was rare in their home. The girls usually tried to work in the evenings, and Clarence was always trying to keep up with his schoolwork. That evening, though, the children were playing with Robert's new train and moving things from one doll bed to the other. They were all laughing and joking together, and Clara loved how well they played.

Clara looked at Albert. "We have a lovely family."

He smiled, his eyes lighting up. "A year ago, I thought my life was over. My wife was dying, and I really thought I'd never know how to smile again. I thank God every day that He brought you into my life and taught me how to smile again. Thank you for teaching me to love again, Clara."

Her eyes met his, misty with unshed tears. "I'm proud to have someone like you to love. I'm happy here, and so are my children."

They joined hands across the table as the children continued to play. They both truly felt blessed to have found one another.

Epilogue

CLARA SAT DOWN TO PUT pen to paper. She hadn't written Elizabeth in over a month, and the younger woman had sent a letter asking if everything was well. Albert had brought it back from town when he'd made a supply run the day before. She looked down at the cradle beside the table and rocked it with her foot as she wrote.

"Dear Elizabeth, I'm so sorry to have worried you. My life is overflowing with goodness. Little Katie is a good baby and a sound sleeper. She's already sleeping through the night every night. I'll start teaching Robert with his older sisters next month. It's hard to believe that I've been here almost a year already. Time certainly does fly when you're happy. Gertie and Natalie took little Robert out to the garden, and they're all weeding for me. I don't want to take her into the sun with as young as she is, so they've taken over my vegetable garden for me. This winter we're going to have a full cellar to choose from. How are things back home? I hope you're still looking for a bride for Eli. He's a good man and deserves to be happy. I'll try to write more often now that the baby is here and healthy. Yours, Clara."

Clara stood and breathed deeply of the late summer air. How could she have doubted that Montana was where she was meant to be?

www.ingramcontent.com/pod-product-compliance
Lightning Source LLC
Chambersburg PA
CBHW031423150726
47989CB00002B/774